More Than
This

clearwater crossing

More Than This

laura peyton roberts

BANTAM BOOKS
NEW YORK • TORONTO • LONDON • SYDNEY • AUCKLAND

RL 5.8, age 12 and up
MORE THAN THIS
A Bantam Book / November 1999

ISBN 0-553-49296-9

Published simultaneously in the United States and Canada.

Bantam Books are published by Bantam Books, a division of Random
House, Inc. Its trademark, consisting of the words "Bantam Books"
and the portrayal of a rooster, is Registered in U.S. Patent and
Trademark Office and in other countries. Marca Registrada. Bantam
Books, 1540 Broadway, New York, New York 10036.

PRINTED IN THE UNITED STATES OF AMERICA

OPM   10 9 8 7 6 5 4 3 2 1

For Lindsay,
who reads them all

Ask and it will be given to you; seek and you will find; knock and the door will be opened to you. For everyone who asks receives; he who seeks finds; and to him who knocks, the door will be opened.

Matthew 7:7-8

One

"Whoops! Excuse me, Mr. Roarke," Nicole Brewster said nervously. "I was just going to get a, uh . . ."

Her boss's small eyes glared, hard with disapproval, and Nicole's breath caught in her chest. Had he seen? Nicole glanced back at her cousin. From the end of the counter where she and Mr. Roarke stood, Gail and her cash register were directly in the boss's line of sight!

He was spying, Nicole realized, dizzy with her own panicked pulse. *He saw everything.*

Despite Nicole's whispered protests, Gail had just given a cute customer more food than he had paid for, pushing it across the counter on a tray Nicole had prepared herself. If there was one unbreakable rule at Wienerageous, the fast-food restaurant where they worked, it was "no free food for anyone, ever"— and Mr. Roarke was the man who had written the rules. Nicole faced him now, her knees weak beneath her as she realized that he had just caught both her and Gail in an act guaranteed to result in dismissal.

1

I can't get fired, Nicole thought frantically. *Mom and Dad will kill me! I haven't even been working a month!*

Less than two weeks before, when Nicole had returned to Missouri after spending the Martin Luther King Day weekend in Hollywood with Leah Rosenthal, Jenna Conrad, and Melanie Andrews, she had fully expected to be grounded. Before she'd left, she'd been blackmailed into helping her younger sister, Heather, toilet-paper a boy's house and, through no fault of Nicole's, their mother had found out. Both girls had been grounded for two weeks, but while Heather had started her sentence immediately, Nicole had been allowed to attend the U.S. Girls modeling contest in California first.

By the time she'd arrived back in Clearwater Crossing, however, her parents had changed their minds. Nicole had been horrified to learn that instead of grounding her they had pulled some strings to get her a job with her cousin Gail, an experience that was supposed to teach her responsibility.

"I, uh, I know how that probably looked," Nicole stammered, fixing her boss with imploring eyes, "but . . ."

But what?

Could she really tell him that this whole mess was Gail's fault? That she had begged her cousin not to give that food away?

Nicole glanced behind her again. Gail stood casually waiting for a customer, completely oblivious to the storm brewing just around the corner.

I could say I was on my way to find him, that I was coming to report Gail's behavior.

In fact, that was the only excuse that might save her. If Mr. Roarke had really seen the whole thing, then he must have seen her arguing with her cousin. Nicole would feel like a rat deserting a sinking ship, but—

"I'll see you in the break room," Mr. Roarke snapped. "Go straight there and wait for me."

Nicole opened her mouth to protest, to try to explain, but he looked so angry that nothing came out. With one last, desperate glance at her cousin, she ran for the break room.

A few seconds later, Mr. Roarke showed up, Gail right behind him. Her cheeks were flushed and her blue eyes looked rounder than usual, but aside from that her face was expressionless. Mr. Roarke motioned the girls into rickety chairs, then stood glowering at them from the greater height that gave him.

"I guess I don't have to tell you that you're both in a lot of trouble," he opened, looking from one to the other.

Nicole withered under his scrutiny, abandoning all hope of offering a defense. Instead she turned to Gail, silently pleading with her cousin to speak for them. If Gail were to take the blame, there was an outside chance that Mr. Roarke would let Nicole off the hook. And it *was* all Gail's fault, after all. . . .

But Gail simply returned his stare with a coolness Nicole would have envied under other circumstances.

"Do you have anything to say for yourselves?" Mr. Roarke asked.

Gail shook her head.

"Gail!" Nicole prompted through clenched teeth.

Her cousin shot her a warning look.

"Very well," said Mr. Roarke. He crossed his arms over his chest and drew himself up to his full, unimpressive height. "Clock out and leave the building immediately."

"But Mr. Roarke!" cried Nicole, finding her voice at last. "Our shift isn't even over. Who's going to work the counter?"

"Let me worry about that," he said coldly. "I want the pair of you out of here now."

"Are we fired?" she wailed. "Please, Mr. Roarke, you can't fire us. My parents will—"

"I'm not going to discuss this any further until I've thought it over," he said to Gail, as if she were the one who had spoken. "Come fifteen minutes early tomorrow and bring your uniforms with you—clean, pressed, and ready to turn in. I'll let you know what I've decided then."

Before Nicole could say another word, he turned and walked out the door, closing it hard behind him.

"Oh my God, we're going to be fired," Nicole moaned. "How could you do this to me, Gail?"

"Just stay calm," Gail told her, rising to her feet. "Nothing's been decided yet."

Nicole jumped up too. "It sounds like it's been decided to me! He told us to turn in our uniforms."

"No, he told us to have them *ready* to turn in."

Nicole stared, unable to believe her cousin's calm. "Gail! When our parents find out about this, they're going to—"

"Ooh," said Gail, shaking her head slightly. "I wouldn't say anything to them yet. Let's just keep this to ourselves until we find out what Roarke says tomorrow." Picking her backpack up off the floor, she slung it over her shoulder, ready to leave without changing into street clothes.

"But you know what he's going to say!"

"No I don't. And neither do you. There's no point panicking prematurely and getting our parents excited for nothing. Just stay calm and I'll see you tomorrow, all right?"

Prematurely? For nothing? Nicole thought disbelievingly, watching her cousin go. *Does she have any concept how much trouble we're in?*

Nicole's hands shook uncontrollably as she retrieved her own backpack. She had thought that nothing in the world could make her go out in public wearing the puffy purple cap, orange-and-pink-striped tunic, and aggressively creased bell-bottoms that were the Wienerageous uniform, but she knew now she'd been wrong. That day all she wanted was to get out of the restaurant as quickly as possible, before Mr. Roarke came back and decided to fire her on the spot.

Taking her coat off a hook, Nicole pulled it on over her tunic and slipped out the break room door, creeping down the hall toward the back exit. She didn't want to run into any of her fellow employees, she didn't want to answer any questions, and she *especially* didn't want to think about what her parents were going to do when they learned what had happened.

Making her escape, she closed the door behind her, knowing she'd barely breathe until she learned her fate the next day.

"Tell me everything," Jenna begged, knowing there couldn't be anything new to tell. Caitlin hadn't spoken to David Altmann since the day before, but that encounter had been so exciting, Jenna still wasn't tired of hearing about it.

"You already know everything," her older sister murmured, blushing.

The girls were in their third-floor bedroom after dinner that Monday night, stretched out on their side-by-side twin beds. Jenna propped herself on one elbow, and Caitlin did the same.

"Yeah, but isn't it great?" Jenna persisted. "I'm so happy for you."

Caitlin's blush increased with her shy smile. "Thanks."

"So, when is he going to call you?"

"I told you. I don't know."

Jenna groaned and flopped onto her back again. "How can you be so patient?" she asked, not really expecting an answer. The uncertainties in David and Caitlin's new relationship were killing her, and she wasn't even involved.

The telephone rang, but both girls ignored it, more interested in continuing their conversation.

Ever since Peter's brother, David, had appeared unexpectedly at church the day before and whisked Caitlin away after services, Jenna had been on pins and needles. At first her almost unbearable curiosity had centered on David's reason for being in Clearwater Crossing, and on what he was saying to Caitlin. Aware of her sister's crush on David, Jenna could only hope he'd come to tell her that he felt the same way. But if he did, then why had he written to Caitlin asking for Mary Beth's college address?

Panic had gripped Jenna next as she'd realized that David might just as easily—no, *more* easily—be in town to gather information on Mary Beth as to visit Caitlin. Poor Caitlin! How would she manage if the love of her life started grilling her for details about her popular older sister? By the time David had dropped Caitlin off at the Conrads' front door, Jenna had been a nervous wreck.

One look at her sister's blissfully happy face, though, had set her mind off in a third direction: Caitlin and David were an item!

But how much of an item? That was the question driving her buggy now. And no matter how many times she made Caitlin go over every detail of the morning she'd spent with David, Jenna couldn't get a satisfactory answer. David had taken Caitlin to brunch, he'd talked of graduating from college later that year, and he'd asked to see her again. That all sounded pretty good, but—

"Caitlin! Jenna!" Mrs. Conrad called from downstairs. "Mary Beth is on the phone."

"Mary Beth!" Caitlin said excitedly, reaching for the cordless on the ledge behind the girls' beds.

"Mary Beth!" Jenna cried, diving to grab it first.

If she couldn't prevent Caitlin from talking to their older sister, then she at least wanted to delay the awful moment as long as possible. What if Mary Beth told Caitlin that Jenna had called her at college to find out if David had ever written? Caitlin would flip if she knew that Jenna had butted into her business again—and Jenna had just calmed her down from the last time.

"Hi, Mary Beth!" Jenna said brightly, frantically trying to think of a way to prevent her from mentioning their previous conversation. "What's new in Nashville?"

"Nothing since the last time I talked to you. I hear all the big news is on your end."

"News?" Jenna repeated weakly. Mary Beth already knew about Caitlin and David—Jenna could tell by her tone. "I guess you've been talking to Mom."

"Like Mom's going to spill that one! No, I've been talking to David. He called to thank me for my help."

Help? Mary Beth hadn't been any help at all! In fact, she'd practically ruined everything by getting in Caitlin's way. Jenna opened her mouth to say so, then abruptly thought better of it. Caitlin was hanging on her every word, her light brown eyes wide with her eagerness to join the conversation.

"Oh," Jenna said at last. "I didn't realize you were *helping*."

"Are you kidding me?" Mary Beth chortled. "I was a lot more help than you and your crack-of-dawn phone calls! Listen, don't ever pursue a career in spying, all right? You'll end up in front of a firing squad your first day."

"What are you talking about?"

"Yeah, what *are* you talking about?" Caitlin echoed curiously.

"Nothing!" Jenna said quickly.

Mary Beth laughed on the other end. "Jenna, I

knew! I was in on it! David did write me a letter—to ask if Caitlin was interested in anyone. I didn't think she was, but I didn't think she was interested in him, either—until you called and let that cat out of the bag."

"I did not!" Jenna protested. "I didn't do anything but—"

"Relax, Columbo. Your secret's safe with me," said Mary Beth, still laughing. "I'm not going to say anything to Caitlin."

"You're not?"

"No. So hand over the phone, all right? I want to talk to Cat."

Jenna passed off the phone in a daze, unable to believe her good luck. Mary Beth wasn't going to tell! She was off the hook!

Falling back into her pillows, she listened in a state of growing euphoria as Caitlin revealed her good news to Mary Beth.

What a relief! And . . . hey! I helped Caitlin out again!

If Jenna hadn't made that clumsy call to Mary Beth, her sister never would have encouraged David to make a move. Not that Jenna could afford to brag, of course.

If Caitlin ever found out that I interfered in her life again, she'd be completely furious.

Hugging her ribs, Jenna listened to Caitlin and Mary Beth talk, overcome with gratitude that Mary

Beth wasn't going to get her in trouble. All the petty spats and disagreements they'd had over the last few months seemed to melt away as if they had never happened.

In fact, at that moment Jenna was certain she had never loved her oldest sister more.

Melanie peered into the dim interior of the big blue mailbox on the corner, but all she saw was the ridged metal ramp the letters slid down. She started to raise her letter to the opening, then abruptly changed her mind and released the door handle. The door slammed shut on squealing hinges, leaving her standing there, undecided, the letter still in her hand.

"What am I doing?" she asked with a groan.

The only answer she got was the sight of her own breath, white in the frosty air.

"I must be crazy."

Did she really want to mail the letter she'd written to Gwen, her mother's only sister? She couldn't even leave it at her house to be picked up with the other mail, because if her father saw it he'd hit the roof. And what if things with her mother's family didn't work out? She could end up even unhappier than she already was.

Melanie turned the envelope over in her gloved hands, trying to make a decision. The bus would be along to pick her up for school any second . . .

"Oh, don't be such a wimp," she told herself, opening the door just long enough to drop her letter through the slot. The moment it clanged shut, however, she whipped it open again, gazing nervously into the darkness.

Gone. And no way to get it back out.

"Great," she groaned, already regretting her hasty decision. "Way to go, Andrews."

What was the big hurry, anyway? She could just as easily have mailed the letter after school. Or the next day.

Or never.

I don't really want to visit Aunt Gwen in Iowa, she thought as she began walking toward her bus stop. *I'm just depressed because things are so lousy here.*

Between her father reneging on rehab and Jesse making it clear that he didn't want anything to do with her, she'd had a rough couple of weeks.

Well, maybe she won't write back, Melanie thought hopefully. *Or if she does, I can always tell her I changed my mind.*

Her aunt was the least of her problems, really. Melanie tried to forget about the letter she'd just mailed as she walked along the paved shoulder of the road toward the bus stop, blind to the rain-soaked fields on either side of her.

I wonder if Jesse will be with Brooke Henderson again today.

She had run into Jesse with the homecoming

12

queen in the student parking lot the day before. Since then, her imagination had been working overtime, making up far more intimate scenarios than were actually likely.

Not that I care *what the two of them get up to*, she thought bitterly.

Not much, anyway.

Two

"Peter! Jenna!" Ben Pipkin yelled. "Here we are!" Jumping to his feet, he waved his friends over to the table he had saved for Eight Prime at the back of the cafeteria. Miguel del Rios and Leah Rosenthal were already there, and so were Melanie and Nicole.

"Hi, guys," Peter Altmann said, dropping his brown bag onto the table and taking a seat on the bench beside Melanie and Nicole. "Sorry we're late."

Jenna sat on Peter's right, making four people on that side of the table to the three on Ben's.

"You're not late," Ben said. "Jesse still isn't here."

"Then *he's* late," Melanie said. "I vote we start without him."

"We're not in that big a hurry, are we?" Miguel asked. "We could wait a few more minutes." He took a sandwich out of his lunch bag and began unwrapping it.

"Let's set up a Thursday-night meeting while we're waiting," Peter suggested. "We had it at Jesse's house last time, so it's someone else's turn anyway."

14

"Good idea," Ben said, nodding enthusiastically. He loved Eight Prime meetings.

The very next second, however, Jenna threw him into a panic. "Why don't we have it at your house, Ben? You haven't hosted a meeting yet."

"At, uh, at *my* house?" he stammered, his heart pumping so fast that little black specks floated before his eyes. "You don't want to have it at *my* house."

Nicole looked up from the carrot stick she was nibbling. "Why not?"

"Well, uh, because . . . um, we're *painting*. Yeah. And the furniture is all covered up. It would be a real problem to use the living room now. I'd have to ask my mom and—"

"Let's just have it at my poolhouse," Melanie offered. "I don't need to ask permission."

"Good! Good idea!" Ben practically shouted.

Everyone stared at him.

"I mean, uh, Melanie's house is a lot nicer anyway."

Leah gave him a strange look, then shrugged. "Do you guys want me to get permission for our sale from Principal Kelly? I don't mind asking."

At the last Eight Prime meeting, the group had decided to sell suckers and carnations as a Valentine's Day fund-raiser. The point of the lunchtime meeting was to refine the plan and assign work.

"Yeah, do that," Nicole told her. "And you'd

better do it fast because Valentine's Day is the Sunday after this one. That's less than two weeks away."

Leah nodded and made a note on the pad in front of her. "So what days am I asking for? Thursday and Friday, or just Friday?"

Ben barely heard the discussion that followed through the blood still whooshing in his ears. Why had he never anticipated that someday Eight Prime would expect to meet at his house? Of course *he* knew that meeting there was impossible, but he should have found a way to let his friends know it too. Now that he had almost succeeded in getting Eight Prime to treat him like a normal member of the group, there was no way he wanted them in the same building with his parents. If his nerdy dad didn't bore them to death with computer stories, his overweight, overbearing mother would probably stuff them all with cookies and try to run the entire meeting. Ben could just imagine her telling Jenna how to take notes or critiquing Peter's accounting. No thanks!

"Hey, Ben," Jesse whispered, sliding in beside him on the bench. "What did I miss?"

"Huh? Oh." With an effort, Ben forced his attention back to the discussion at the table. "There's an Eight Prime meeting at Melanie's house this Thursday."

Jesse rolled his eyes. "Her house *again*?"

"And Leah's going to get permission for the sale

from Principal Kelly," Ben added guiltily, wondering if Jesse thought Ben should have taken a turn at hosting the meeting too.

"So, who wants to look into buying the suckers?" Peter asked. "Somebody should get some prices before we meet again on Thursday."

"I'll do it!" Ben volunteered. "I'll get prices for the flowers, too."

"You don't have to do everything, Ben," said Jenna. "Why don't we split the work up?"

"It's already split up. Leah's getting permission, Melanie's holding the meeting, and you and Peter always do everything. It's my turn to do something big for a change."

"Pricing the suckers is big enough," Melanie told him.

"Yeah, Ben," echoed Nicole. "Let a girl pick out the flowers."

"You think I can't buy flowers?" Ben demanded. "Besides, there's nothing to pick out. We already said we were getting carnations, so now it's simple dollars and cents."

"There's nothing simple about sense," Miguel muttered.

Nicole and Jesse looked ready to agree with him, but Peter took Ben's side. "I'm sure Ben is perfectly capable of getting prices on both the suckers and flowers."

His eyes met Ben's uneasily. "If you really want to."

"Yes! I do!" Ben insisted. "Trust me, I can handle it."

"Should I write that down?" Jenna asked, her pen poised over the pad she took the meeting notes in.

"Yes," said Ben.

No one else answered.

Leah raised a finger to point across the cafeteria. "Hey, Nicole, Courtney's coming over."

"She is?" Nicole turned her head to look, then whipped it back around, a sour expression on her face. "No, she isn't."

"Who's that girl she's with?" Jenna asked.

"No one." Nicole snapped a celery stick so hard that bits of juice sprayed across the table. "Her name's Emily Dooley."

"Okay, so write it down," Ben said, leaning across the table to recall Jenna's attention to the matter at hand. He pointed to her pad. "I'm in charge of buying the stuff."

"Of checking the prices," Melanie corrected.

"Don't worry," Ben said confidently. "I know what I'm doing."

And suddenly he couldn't wait to prove it. Between his expertise with the Internet and all the time he had on his hands, he was sure to find Eight Prime the best prices they'd ever seen.

Nicole snuck in the back door of Wienerageous, afraid to come through the dining room at the front of the small restaurant. She was afraid to come in through the back, for that matter, but it wasn't as if she had a choice. Mr. Roarke would be waiting for them, and it was time for her and Gail to hear his decision regarding their fates. The paper bag containing her carefully washed and pressed uniform rustled in her arms as Nicole traveled the short hall to the break room, nearly running in her eagerness not to encounter anyone who might ask embarrassing questions.

The door to the break room was closed but not locked. Nicole threw it open and hurried inside, only to find Gail and Mr. Roarke already there. She skidded to a halt near the doorway as both of them turned to stare from the table where they sat.

Gail appeared as coolly immaculate as always, her pale skin just barely flushed pink and her shining black hair falling smooth and straight to her shoulders. Someone who didn't know her probably wouldn't even have noticed the slight trace of desperation in her eyes.

Mr. Roarke, on the other hand, seemed just barely under control. His thinning hair looked as if he'd combed it with a rake, his cheeks were nearly purple, and even his puny mustache bristled with the strength of his convictions. Gail's carefully folded uniform lay on the table between them, untouched by either one.

"Wait in the hall, Nicole," he snapped. "I'm talking to Gail now."

"But, um—"

"Close the door behind you."

Nicole backed out of the room, quietly shutting the door on the scary scene inside. Was Gail being fired? Was Mr. Roarke about to do the same to her?

Clasping her paper bag to her chest, Nicole barely noticed how she crushed her mushroom cap as she paced nervously up and down the short hall. She could hear Eric and Ajax out in the kitchen, slamming the pans around and laughing, unaware of the scene unfolding in the break room.

What I wouldn't give to be in the kitchen too! she thought. She couldn't believe she was nostalgic for Ajax's obnoxious company, but even chopping a ton or two of onions seemed like a good time compared to her present agony. She wondered if any of the other employees knew how much trouble she and Gail were in. And, of course, getting fired was nothing compared to the trouble she'd be in at home. She had barely slept the night before, worrying about what her parents would do.

I'm not saying good-bye, she decided, still pacing. *As soon as I'm done talking to Mr. Roarke, I'm out of here.*

It would be too humiliating to face her fellow workers and explain what had happened; even more humiliating if she started to cry, which seemed almost certain. Anxious tears already burned behind her lids, tying knots inside her throat. If Mr. Roarke even looked at her sideways she'd be blubbering faster than—

The break room door burst open and Mr. Roarke strode out, heading straight toward the kitchen. She stared after him a moment, wondering if he had somehow failed to see her down at the dark end of the hall. Or could he have forgotten she was waiting? A hundred questions in her mind, Nicole sprinted to the doorway.

"There you are," Gail greeted her calmly, reaching for the uniform on the table. "Shut that door and suit up. We're on the clock in five minutes."

"We're . . . we're *what*?" Nicole demanded, unable to believe her ears. "We're not fired? What happened?"

Gail shrugged. "He changed his mind."

"Just like that? I don't believe you."

"Well, it's true, so put on your uniform and let's go."

But Nicole remained frozen in place. Gail stepped past her to lock the door and began getting dressed for work.

"I just want to know what happened," Nicole insisted. "What about Roarke's Rules? What about no free food for anyone, ever?"

"We cut a deal—plus I promised not to take food ever again."

"What kind of deal?"

"It's . . . nothing. It's so stupid."

"I'm not getting dressed until you tell me what it is."

Gail sighed. "I just have to go out with him."

"You mean, like, on a *date*?" Nicole asked, revolted.

"Yes. And don't say a word about this to anyone, because no one's supposed to know. Mr. Roarke will have a cow if anyone here finds out—and if our parents do, that kind of defeats the whole purpose."

"You mean you're *going*?"

"It's that or we're both out of here. I don't see how I have a choice." Gail pointed at Nicole's uniform bag, reminding her to start moving. "I mean, you wanted me to get us out of this. Right?"

"Right! Of course!" Nicole dumped the contents of her bag out on the table and hurriedly began dressing.

I'm not fired! I can't believe it!

Even her gaudy Wienerageous togs seemed less horrendous as she pulled them on with trembling hands. Of course, it *was* kind of gross for Gail, but under the circumstances, Nicole couldn't help thinking her cousin had gotten off easy.

Not that I'd want to go out with him, she thought, suppressing a shudder. But fair was fair. Besides, Gail

22

was such an expert kiss-up that Mr. Roarke would never guess what the girls really thought of him.

"I mean, it's just one date," Nicole added, bubbling over with relief. "One evening to put this whole thing behind us? I think that's pretty good."

"I guess. I just want to get it over with before I have a chance to think about it. We're going to dinner tomorrow night."

"Yeah, that's what I'd do too," said Nicole, incredibly grateful that she was only speaking hypothetically. "Let's see. Tomorrow's Wednesday, so by Thursday you'll be free of the whole situation. Just like it never happened."

"Unless Neil finds out," Gail said darkly. "I suppose he'd understand, though, if I told him the whole story."

"You haven't told him already?"

"What for? It's not exactly something I'm proud of."

"No." Nicole stopped pinning on her hat, distracted by the mention of Gail's boyfriend. "Hey, Gail, why does Neil call you Jelly, anyway?"

Gail sighed. "It's just . . . never mind. Are we working or what?"

"I thought you were going to clean out my refrigerator," Charlie Johnson said, gripping the TV tray in front of his shabby recliner and leaning forward to peer at Jesse. The old man's hands were a road map of gnarled veins and swollen knuckles, but his sharp blue eyes were as steady as ever.

"Do you *want* your refrigerator cleaned out?" Jesse asked without moving a muscle.

"No."

"Then what's the problem?"

"I'm waiting for you to tell me."

"Huh?" Jesse tried to sit straighter on Charlie's brown sofa, but the old cushions were so broken down that the best he could manage was an upright slouch. "There's no problem."

"Come on, Jesse. I'm old, not stupid. Something's eating you or you wouldn't have come over."

"Nice! I came to help you."

"And *are* you helping me?" Charlie asked. "Because I'd have sworn you were just moping on my couch."

"I'm not moping," Jesse began, but another skeptical look from Charlie made him change his story. "Well, all right. Maybe I am. There's just this girl I like and—"

"I should have known," Charlie said with a flicker of a grin. "Let me guess: She doesn't even know you exist."

"Oh, she knows," said Jesse, not bothering to hide his bitterness. "She dumped me two weeks ago."

Charlie shook his silver head. "Worse than I thought."

"It's just that I thought I knew her and instead it

24

turns out I have absolutely no idea what goes on in her mind. I mean, first she wants nothing to do with me, then she practically throws herself at my feet, and now she's acting like I'm invisible."

Charlie shook his head again, this time with sympathy. "Never understood women myself." He gestured with one arm at the lonely house around them. "Obviously."

Jesse heaved himself off the sofa. "Yeah. Well, what's the point? Who needs them, anyway?"

But driving home later, he knew he was the biggest liar on Earth. If he really didn't need Melanie, then why did he want her so bad?

"What I need is a drink," he told the empty interior of his BMW as he drove through the cloudy twilight.

That had been his secret reason for visiting Charlie that Tuesday. Once a professional football player, Charlie had let alcohol ruin his life. When Jesse had been forced into helping him as a consequence of getting caught with liquor at school, Charlie had warned him clearly about the danger of following too closely in his footsteps. Every once in a while, though, it didn't hurt to drop in for a reminder.

Except that I'm fine now, Jesse thought.

He had more or less made up his mind back in December to quit drinking. Everyone was giving him such a hard time about it, and besides, he had promised his coach that he already had. On top

25

of that, Melanie had some sort of inexplicable aversion to alcohol, so he really had to watch himself around her. He hadn't touched a drop since before Christmas Eve, when she'd unexpectedly asked him to drive her to Iowa, and he'd rarely even thought of drinking the whole time they'd been together.

But ever since she'd dumped him, he thought of it most of the day. There was no doubt that if it weren't for the lock on the Joneses' liquor cabinet, he'd have drunk until he passed out the night Melanie left him and went to California. He hadn't had the opportunity, though, and somehow he'd managed to hold out since then, despite the fact that seeing her felt like a knife through his heart. His only consolation was the promise he'd made himself on the day they'd broken up: that when Melanie finally realized what she'd thrown away, she could beg all she wanted and not get him back.

The thing was, he hadn't actually expected that day to come. So when Melanie had started following him around the minute she got back from Hollywood, he hadn't known what to think. Did she like him? Was she messing with him? Or did she just miss all the attention from the former biggest member of her fan club?

Jesse groaned with frustration as he pulled into his driveway. Whatever the attraction had been, she seemed to be over it now. Just when he had actually been considering forgiving her, the ice queen's true colors had blossomed again. At the Eight Prime meeting that noon, Melanie had acted for all the world as if there had been only seven people at the table.

"Not that I care," Jesse said, slamming his car door.

And if he did, he would never admit it. There was no way he'd let Melanie Andrews make a fool of him a second time.

The phone began ringing as Jesse climbed the stairs. He still hadn't reached his bedroom when his twelve-year-old stepsister, Brittany, started screaming. "Jesse! Telephone!"

Melanie?

Jesse sprinted to his extension and snatched it up. "Hello?"

"Jesse!" his mother said. "How *are* you? I'm so glad to have caught you!"

As excited as he was to hear from her, he couldn't suppress his first sarcastic thought: *So glad to have caught me instead of Dad or Elsa, you mean.* His parents' divorce had been bitter enough, but since his father had remarried they went out of their way not to speak to each other. His mother almost never telephoned for fear of having to deal with her ex.

"Hi, Mom! What's up?"

"Good news. I'm coming to Clearwater Crossing."

"You're . . . *what*? Now? How come?"

"To see you, of course." His mother's voice grew a little tentative. "Aren't you glad?"

"Of course I'm *glad*. It's just . . . if you came during a vacation, I'd have more free time. Or why not have me come out there? There's nothing to see in Missouri."

"How would I know when I've never been there? You spent most of your life in Malibu. Now I want to see where you live."

Jesse sighed. "All right. If that's the only way."

At least he'd get to see her, and since his father would never let him miss school to go to California anyway, maybe having her come to Missouri was best. Besides, it *could* be kind of fun to show her around. "When are you coming?"

"Friday. I'm staying at the Lakehouse Lodge. Is that a nice place?"

Jesse had never heard of it. "It's probably as nice as anywhere else around here. Do you need me to pick you up at the airport?"

"No, I'm renting a car. But let's have dinner Friday night, okay?"

"Sure. All right."

"Call me at the hotel when you get home from school. I should be there by then."

Jesse found a pencil on his desk to write down the number she gave him.

"It'll be great to see you, Jesse."

28

"You too," he said, meaning it. No one else understood him the way his mother did. No one else had ever made him feel half as good about himself.

As far as Jesse was concerned, once his mother was in town, Melanie and everyone else could go jump in the lake.

Three

"Courtney, wait!" Nicole ran to catch her friend in the CCHS quad, determined to take advantage of the fact that Courtney was alone.

Courtney slowed her steps, then reluctantly stopped and turned around. Her red hair frizzed around her face, and her green eyes snapped with barely suppressed irritation. "What do you want, Nicole?"

"What do I *want*? I thought we were best friends."

Courtney shrugged, drawing her coat around her more tightly. The temperature had plummeted that Wednesday compared to the last few days, but Nicole barely noticed as she faced down her fickle friend. So what if she'd gone on a trip that Courtney hadn't been invited on? And was it her fault if Courtney's boyfriend, Jeff Nguyen, had decided to end things a few days before Nicole left? Nicole had done her best to be a good, sympathetic friend, but Courtney expected the moon, as usual. And while Nicole had been feeling guilty, doing her best to make up, Courtney had taken revenge too far.

"What's the story with Emily Dooley?" Nicole blurted out angrily. "Don't you remember our deal?"

"Our deal?" Courtney cocked a finely plucked brow. "Why don't you remind me."

"I told you in seventh grade that I wouldn't put up with that girl! It's me or her, Courtney. That was the deal."

"Deal? No, I'm pretty sure that was your spoiled little ultimatum."

"I won't—" Nicole began furiously.

"You don't get to make the rules anymore, Nicole. If you were ever around, maybe your tantrum would carry more weight, but I'm sick of playing second fiddle to the God Squad."

"What's that supposed to mean?"

"Just that you'll be sorry if you make me choose. At least Emily has time for me."

"You know I hate that girl!" Nicole shouted, near tears.

Courtney stared her down scornfully. "Oh, grow up, Nicole. You don't even know her. And unless you want to join us for lunch, you're only making me late."

She stalked off across the emptying quad, leaving Nicole blinking hard in her wake.

What's happening to us? thought Nicole, running a hand across her eyes. She and Courtney had been friends for so long that she couldn't even imagine life without her. *I don't want to imagine it.*

But their friendship had been slowly unraveling since school had started that fall, and maybe it had been Nicole's fault. A little.

After all, she *had* been spending a lot of time with Eight Prime—the God Squad, as Courtney insisted on calling them. On the other hand, when Courtney had been with Jeff, Nicole had spent plenty of time alone, and Courtney hadn't seen anything wrong with that.

That's because it's Court's way or the highway, Nicole thought, anger swelling inside her again. *And that's the way it's always been.*

She felt like marching into the cafeteria and giving Courtney and Emily both a piece of her mind. Her eyes narrowed. Her fists found her hips.

This is starting to look like seventh grade all over again!

Melanie was headed toward the bus stop after classes when she caught sight of Jesse standing alone at the edge of the student parking lot.

She averted her eyes, not wanting him to know she had seen him, but her steps slowed involuntarily.

What is he doing? she wondered. The way he was hanging around made her think he was waiting for somebody.

Brooke, maybe? But the homecoming queen was nowhere in sight.

What if he's waiting for me?

Considering how completely he'd ignored her at the Eight Prime meeting the day before, it was hard to imagine why he would be, but back when Jesse had been chasing her he'd used to post himself about there, waiting to pounce when she walked by. What if he *was* waiting for her?

Melanie hesitated another second, then changed direction slightly. She wasn't going to walk right to him, but if he wanted to meet her halfway she'd make his walk a little shorter. Her heart beat faster and her mouth grew dry as she neared the halfway point and peeked his way again.

He was looking right at her. It was impossible to pretend their eyes hadn't met. Melanie forced a weak smile, hoping she wasn't making an even bigger fool of herself than Jesse already had. He stared a moment, stonefaced, then abruptly left his spot and strode toward her across the lawn.

"You waiting for someone?" she asked.

"No. Like who?"

"I don't know. Like Brooke?"

He rolled his eyes, a pained expression on his face. "Jump to conclusions, why don't you? I just gave her a ride yesterday. Not that it's any of your business."

"I didn't say it was."

They faced each other down in the cold winter air, Jesse's ears bright pink with the chill. It seemed like such a little-boy thing to forget a hat that Melanie suddenly longed to reach up and cup her gloved hands around them. Maybe pull his face down to hers . . .

"My mom is coming on Friday," he said suddenly. "She's staying for a week."

"She's coming here? All the way from California?"

"It's not that far away," Jesse said irritably.

"I know. But she's never been here before."

Her remark had been innocent enough, but Jesse's blue eyes darkened angrily. "What's that supposed to mean?"

"I wasn't trying to insult you. I only—"

"I suppose your little Hollywood boyfriend is going to fly out here every weekend," he said sarcastically. "Have you even heard from him once?"

"You mean Brad? No, I haven't heard from him, because I didn't give him my number."

She couldn't believe he was throwing Brad in her face again. The only reason she'd even told him about the incredibly cute guy she'd met in California was because she was trying to explain how she'd come to realize she liked Jesse better. She'd *thought* she liked him better, anyway. Now she was sorry she'd ever mentioned it.

"Ha! It must have been real hot and heavy if he didn't even ask for your phone number."

"For your information, he did ask. I decided not to give it to him."

"Why?" Jesse said suspiciously.

Because I was stupid enough to believe I was in love with you! Why did she and Jesse have to cover the same ground over and over? Didn't he ever listen to anything she told him?

"You know what?" she said angrily. "I don't even remember anymore. I *should* have given Brad my number. I should have run away with him and never come back!"

"That would have been fine with me."

The words stung, but Melanie was too furious to flinch. "I wasn't asking your permission."

Then, before he could say another rude thing, she spun around and stalked toward the bus stop. She had better things to do than trade insults with Jesse Jones.

She knew she ought to, anyway.

"Hurry up, Jesse!" Brittany yelled from downstairs. "Dinner!"

After the fight he'd just had with Melanie, the last thing Jesse needed was a dose of his so-called family. Between the bad mood he was already in and the fact that his father and Elsa were both in immature snits about his mother's impending visit, dinner that night was sure to be even worse torture than usual.

"*Jesse!*" Brittany screamed again.

"Leave him alone, dear," Elsa said, her voice pitched in a way that was certain to reach him. "You did your best. It's not your fault if he's too rude to join us."

His stepmother's sarcasm only added five minutes to the amount of time he intended to make them wait. He stretched out on his bed, letting the time slip by, thinking of Melanie. When he finally dragged himself downstairs, everyone else was done with their salads and starting on the main course.

"If you can't be bothered to come when you're called, next time you'll skip dinner altogether," Dr. Jones said as Jesse pulled out a chair.

"Why wait? I'll be happy to skip it right now."

"You might have had the courtesy to tell me that before I bothered making all this food," Elsa complained, as if they didn't all know the housekeeper had done everything but serve it.

"Sit down," his father growled.

Jesse dropped into the chair across from Brittany's and began helping himself to some pot roast.

"I'm not going to put up with much more of your attitude, Jesse. Ever since you found out your mother was coming to visit, you've been impossible to be around."

"I haven't even *been* around." *And you're the one who's impossible*, he felt like adding. Instead he speared a baby carrot, pretending he was on some hot, distant island while he chewed it.

"I just don't know what Beth is thinking," Dr.

Jones grumbled to Elsa. "What in the world made her think she'd be welcome here?"

Jesse forced himself to swallow. "It's a free country," he said through gritted teeth. "I guess she can go where she likes. Besides, she's staying in a hotel, so what's the big deal?"

"I'm paying for it. *That's* the big deal," Dr. Jones shot back. "To hear your mother tell it, she's so poor she can't even get by without alimony. Then she turns around and wastes it like this. It's bad enough I have to pay for her rent and food and everything else. I shouldn't have to cover her vacations too."

"Or if you do, they should at least be somewhere far, far away," Elsa said with a phony giggle.

Dr. Jones smiled appreciatively, but Jesse felt sick to his stomach. Didn't they realize this was his *mother* they were talking about? Not to mention how it felt to find out that his father considered a trip to see him wasted money. Jesse looked disbelievingly from one to the other, ignoring Brittany completely.

"I wish she'd remarry," Elsa said. "Sending that check every month is like making payments on a broken-down car you don't even own anymore."

"Worse," said her husband. "At least you can scrap a car."

The duo laughed as if Dr. Jones were Billy Crystal and Robin Williams rolled into one. Jesse scraped back his chair and shot them both lethal looks before abandoning his dinner.

If they don't have the sense to shut up, I don't have to listen to them, he thought as he slammed his bedroom door. He wasn't hungry anyway. Not anymore.

Grabbing his trigonometry text out of his backpack, he carried it to the table under his window. He reached to turn on his desk lamp, then froze, arrested by the scene before him.

Outside, the tiniest bit of snow drifted gently through the darkness, catching the light of an early moon. Snowflakes settled on the brittle grass and dusted the trees across the street, making everything seem brighter than it was. Jesse felt his breathing gradually return to normal at the sight of so much beauty.

Then his door burst open and the snowy scene outside disappeared in the glare of the overhead light. All his window reflected was his own angry face and, behind that, Brittany's, small and half lost in his doorway.

He whirled around in his desk chair, furious. "What are you doing? Did you hear an invitation? Because I didn't even hear a knock."

Brittany seemed frightened but she held her ground. "You didn't have any lights on, Jesse. How was I supposed to know you were in here in the dark?"

"So you thought you'd sneak around in my room while I was somewhere else? Let me catch you at that just *once*, Brittany—"

"I wasn't sneaking around. I was only looking for you."

"What bull! You just said you didn't even think I was in here."

Some corner of Jesse's mind realized he probably wasn't being reasonable, but it wasn't a corner he cared to explore. Between the situation with Melanie and the state of affairs with his parents, he was simply aching for a fight—and here was Brittany, a custom-made target.

"Guy, Jesse," she whimpered, shuffling stocking feet. Her legs were still little-girl skinny, pale beneath her Catholic-school jumper. "I only wanted to talk to you. You don't have to jump down my throat."

She pushed a strand of blond hair behind one protruding ear and stood regarding him warily. In contrast to the icy blue of Elsa's, Brittany's eyes were meltingly brown—the only obvious feature the pair didn't have in common.

"If you wanted to talk, you should have done it while I was downstairs," he said nastily. "Your mother certainly had plenty to say."

"My mom's afraid of your mom, that's all."

"That's ridiculous. All your mom is afraid of is

that her gravy train'll run out and she'll have to do something drastic, like make her own decisions, or even get a job. All your mom's afraid of is my dad dying without leaving her every cent he's ever earned."

"That's not true!" The tears began running past Brittany's freckled nose, but Jesse didn't let up.

"It is, and you're just like her. You make me sick the way you mince around here in your private-school uniforms, like you're too good to go to public school with the rest of us plebes."

"I didn't *pick* Sacred Heart," she said, crying harder. "I wanted—"

"Nobody cares what you wanted! Now get out of my room."

Brittany gaped at him, eyes streaming, then turned and ran. He could hear her choking back sobs as she rushed down the hall in the direction of her own room.

For a moment, he almost felt guilty. Weren't his shots at Elsa just as low as Elsa's at his mom?

On the other hand, Elsa didn't have to live with his mom, and Brittany had been asking for trouble the moment she'd opened his door.

She should just stay on her side of the house and I'll stay on mine.

If he could only put his dad and Elsa in the other two corners, then everyone would be happy.

40

*　*　*

Jenna hummed contentedly as she settled onto her bed with a brand-new pad and pen. They'd just had her favorite meat-loaf dinner, and now Caitlin was downstairs watching TV with the younger girls, leaving Jenna the room to herself. For the first time in months she wasn't fighting with any of her sisters. She was in love, Caitlin was in love, Valentine's Day was right around the corner. . . .

Life was just generally great.

Uncapping her pen with her teeth, she scrawled two words at the top of a fresh pink page: *Valentine's Day*.

This Valentine's Day, her first one as a couple with Peter, was going to be the most completely romantic day ever—Jenna would make sure of that. Snuggling further into her pillows, she held her pen poised over her pad.

Should she and Peter go out to dinner? Where? *Maybe I should let him decide*.

Still, it was fun to think about. She considered the possibilities a moment longer, then wrote *Dinner* at the top of the page. They'd definitely go to dinner somewhere.

Good. Now what type of present should I get him?

She wanted it to be something special, and the last thing she wanted was a repeat of Christmas, when all her plans had gone wrong and she'd been scrambling for a gift until the very last minute. *No, this time I'm going to be organized!*

Gift, she wrote, underlining it three times.

I wonder what he's going to get me?

Not that she was expecting something expensive, just a little something she could keep, something from the heart. . . .

Jenna's pen dropped to her pad again. *I can't wait!* she wrote excitedly.

Four

I'll show Eight Prime they can count on me! Ben thought, shuffling happily through the order forms on the cafeteria table in front of him. His congealing chili sat to one side, nearly as forgotten as his friend Mark Foster.

"I still don't understand what you're doing," Mark complained from across the table. "If you're not going to fill those out, why don't you put them away?"

"I'm just checking," Ben said importantly.

"Checking what? All I see is a bunch of blank printouts."

"That's what I'm checking."

Later that evening, at the Eight Prime meeting, Ben would be presenting the results of the research he'd done on the Internet: every product, every price, even the delivery schedules. He wanted each page to be in order, each fact on the tip of his tongue. When he finished describing his work to Eight Prime, he wanted everyone in the room to think just one thing: Ben Pipkin really knew how to take charge of a situation.

43

"Well, put that stuff away or I'm going to the computer lab," said Mark. "This is getting boring."

"All right, all right. I was nearly finished anyway." He began gathering up his papers just as Angela Maldonado walked past the table.

"Boy, I'm glad I'm not in whatever class that is!" she said, pointing to his paperwork. "What's all that for?"

Ben tapped the last few pages back into his stack, making a perfect rectangle. "This? Just some stuff I got off the Internet. Eight Prime is having a Valentine's Day fund-raiser next week, and *I'm* in charge of ordering everything."

"Congratulations," Angela said, looking perhaps more amused than impressed. There was a hint of laughter in her brown eyes, and the corner of her mouth by the beauty mark twitched into a dimple. "What are you guys raising money for this time?"

"Gas and maintenance. Plus we had Kurt Englbehrt's name painted on the bus, and we bought the Junior Explorers a bunch of new sports stuff. We're kind of broke."

"Those little kids are so cute. What's the fund-raiser going to be?"

Ben described Eight Prime's idea, his mind half on what he was saying and half on the pink cashmere skirt only inches from his shoulder. Was everything Angela wore really as soft as it looked?

"Well, good luck. I promise to buy a sucker," Angela said when he'd finished. "I'll see you around, all right?"

"See you." Ben sighed, watching her long curls bounce as she walked off across the cafeteria. He knew better than anyone that a pretty cheerleader like Angela couldn't be expected to give a nerd like him the time of day. Still, ever since he'd met her at the Eight Prime pumpkin sale, she'd not only regularly acknowledged his existence, she acted almost as if she considered him a friend. . . .

"Yeah, dream on," Mark snorted, jolting Ben back to reality. "I know what *you're* thinking."

Ben felt the blood pound in his cheeks as he faced his forgotten companion. "I doubt it."

"She's a little out of your league, isn't she? Besides, rumor is she's dating one of the basketball players."

"Not that I'm interested," Ben said, working to keep his voice cool, "but which one?"

Mark loosed a bark of laughter that made Ben cringe.

"No, you're not interested," he said knowingly. "Not very."

Nicole checked to make sure the short hallway was empty, then hurried to lock the break room door behind her, knowing she and Gail had only a few minutes before Mr. Roarke expected them to start their Thursday shift.

"So what happened?" she asked breathlessly. "Was it totally awful?"

Gail cracked the merest shadow of a smile as she pulled on her blue work pants. "This *is* Mr. Dork we're talking about. Did you think it could be some other way?"

"Ugh," Nicole said with a shudder. "I felt so sorry for you last night. Where did you two end up going?"

Gail rolled her eyes. "That was the only good part about the whole thing. Roarke wanted to be spotted with me even less than I wanted to be seen with him. I guess it's pretty obvious when you think about it. There's the age difference, not to mention the whole employer-employee thing. . . ."

Nicole nodded impatiently, wishing her cousin would hurry up and get to the good part.

"I had to meet him at the Mapleton Mall parking lot so my parents wouldn't see him pick me up," Gail continued. "And he took me to this hole-in-the-wall diner all the way out in Cave Creek."

"Sounds romantic," said Nicole with a roll of her eyes.

"That's the most pathetic part of all. I think he actually thought it was! Sneaking around, stolen love—I don't know. The guy has the emotional IQ of an ant. I can't belive he's thirty-four."

"He's thirty-*four*?" Nicole slapped a hand over her mouth as her words rang out in the small break room.

She'd guessed Mr. Roarke could be as old as thirty, or even thirty-one, but thirty-*four*. . . .

Lowering her hand, she lowered her voice as well. "I mean . . . yuck!"

Gail shook her head, then pinned on her uniform cap. "He brought me flowers, as if I could take them home. Then, after two cheese steaks completely smothered in onions, he actually tried to kiss me good-night."

"I'm sick!" Nicole gasped. "How gross!"

Gail giggled. "Yeah, well. I said he *tried*. He's probably never seen anyone duck that fast."

She finished with her cap and stood waiting for a partially dressed Nicole. "You know what part was saddest? He didn't even seem to realize I was only there because he blackmailed me. I think he actually believed we were on a real date or something."

Nicole fought back another shudder. "At least it's over!" she said sympathetically. Gail had endured one awful night, but no harm had been done and no one else ever needed to know. If that was the price of not being fired, it actually seemed pretty cheap.

"It's not exactly *over*," Gail said. "I have to go out with him again Friday night."

"What? I thought it was just one date!"

For the first time that afternoon, a little real emotion showed through Gail's perfect façade. "So did I, and I don't think it's fair. But what am I going to do? He kind of has me, you know?"

"Yeah," Nicole said slowly. He had them both, actually. "So are you going?"

"Unless you have a better idea."

"Not really," she said with a sigh of secret relief. She felt sorry for Gail, of course, but the whole thing *was* her cousin's fault. The least she could do was bail them both out of the mess she'd made.

And if that meant one more date with Mr. Roarke, well . . . then that was the way it had to be.

"Everyone's here but Nicole," Melanie announced to the noisy group in her poolhouse. "And she's nearly ten minutes late."

"Oh! Oh, I forgot to tell you!" Jenna said, looking up from the cushioned chaise she was sharing with Peter. "Nicole called me and said she'd be late. She said we should start without her."

"All right," Melanie said, biting back all the other, more sarcastic, replies that came to mind. Why, for example, had Nicole called Jenna instead of her when the meeting was at her house? Better still, why did Jenna have to monopolize every second of Peter's time during what was supposed to be a group event? And, at the very least, couldn't Jenna have given her the message earlier? "I guess we'll get started, then. If everyone else is ready."

Leah was already on the sofa, and Jesse had one of the Hawaiian-print chairs. Miguel grabbed a Coke off the bar at the back of the room and walked over to join Leah, while Ben wiped hands covered with greasy potato-chip crumbs across the front of his jeans.

"I'm ready!" he called, as if that were the key to the entire meeting. "I have all of my papers right here."

Grabbing hurriedly at the thick stack of sheets he'd set on the bar, he got only half a grip on them before starting back toward the center of the room. The papers slid off the edge of the counter, then fell backward out of his hand, scattering all over the floor.

"Wait!" Ben cried, dropping to his knees. "Nobody touch! I've got them all in order."

"Sure you do," Jesse muttered, twirling a rubber band around one finger.

"While he's doing that," said Leah, checking to make sure Jenna had begun taking notes, "I can tell you what Principal Kelly said."

Peter leaned forward. "Oh, you talked to him."

"Yes, and I have good news and bad news. The good news is we can hold our sale at school next Thursday and Friday."

"That's great news!" Jenna cried. "What can be bad about that?"

"The Associated Student Body is having a Valentine's Day sale too," Miguel answered for her. "They're selling heart-shaped boxes of chocolates."

"Perfect," Melanie groaned. "The student council has chocolate and all we have is suckers? They're going to kill us."

A knock sounded on the poolhouse door and Nicole let herself in, a hat pulled low over half-wet hair. "Sorry I'm late," she said. "Did I miss anything?"

"Only the fact that we're about to lose our shirts," said Jesse, motioning to her to sit next to him. "The ASB is selling chocolates for Valentine's Day."

"Oh, no. Well, we don't have to go through with our sale. Right?" Nicole dropped into a chair and looked around at the group. "I mean, we're not married to the idea. We haven't even bought the stuff yet."

"That's true," said Peter. "It might be better just to write this off and come up with something else. Another car wash or something."

"No more car washes," Jenna said quickly.

"Especially not in this weather," Leah agreed. "We'd be better off with another pancake breakfast."

"What if we did French toast this time?" Melanie suggested. "That would be different."

"No! No, wait!" Ben cried, running into the center of the group with an armload of rumpled papers. Pages from his once-neat stack stuck out every which way, half of them upside down. "I still think we ought to do this."

"I don't," said Miguel. "In case you've forgotten, we don't have any money. If we put in our own personal money and the sale flops, then what? We lose it, that's what. It's too risky."

"It's *not* risky!" Ben insisted, his voice rising to a squeak. "You have to let me show you guys this stuff before you decide."

Dropping to his knees beside the glass coffee table, Ben found a paper in the stack and held it up like a manifesto. His hands were shaking with agitation, and the deep breaths he took didn't seem to make him less nervous.

"Go ahead, Ben," Melanie said, feeling sorry for him.

Ben stood up, still clutching his paper. "This is a breakdown of all the different online stores I found and what they're selling. If the ASB is selling boxes of chocolate, they're going to be what? Five dollars, at least? I can get red heart-shaped suckers for twenty cents. If we turn around and sell them for a dollar . . ."

"That's a pretty good profit," said Jesse, sitting straighter in his chair.

"I don't think we can charge a dollar for a twenty-cent sucker," Jenna protested with a worried expression.

"Why not?" asked Nicole. "When it's for charity, no one expects a good deal."

"They don't expect to get ripped off, either," Leah said, taking Jenna's side.

"Well, even if we sell them for fifty cents . . . ," Ben began.

"Seventy-five," Jesse countered.

"My *point* is," Ben continued, "we'll buy them cheap, way undersell the ASB, and still make a good profit. People who don't have the money for a box of chocolates can still buy a sucker *and* a flower from us."

"Yeah, what about the flowers?" Leah asked. "You're not thinking of buying those over the Internet?"

"Why not?" Ben asked, visibly more confident now that his sucker argument seemed to have carried the day.

"How are they going to ship flowers without water?" Nicole asked skeptically. "They won't be fresh."

"They're *guaranteed* fresh, Nicole. Flowers get shipped all over the country every day. How do you think they get to the florists?"

"He has a point," said Miguel.

"What do they cost?" Leah asked.

"The same place that has the suckers sells a bundle of twenty-five carnations for twelve fifty. We could get 'em even cheaper if we had a wholesale license, but that's still only fifty cents a piece."

"We could *definitely* sell those for a dollar," said Melanie.

"Okay, so someone gets a sucker and flower for a dollar fifty," Jenna said. "That's pretty good."

"A dollar seventy-five," Jesse insisted.

"Whatever," Melanie said impatiently. "It's still good."

"The ASB won't be able to touch us," Ben predicted. "Not at those prices. And you know what? Half the people who buy chocolates will still probably buy a flower. Maybe even a sucker. Why not?"

"Ben's right," Melanie said, earning a grateful smile from Captain Internet. "Besides, we aren't laying out that much money. I think we ought to do it."

A long discussion followed, with everyone trying to arrive at the best estimate of the number of items they expected to sell. Nicole thought they ought to buy conservatively on the flowers, since they yielded much less profit than the suckers. Ben disagreed, pointing out that they had to sell only half of what they bought to break even and everything after that was profit. Melanie reminded the group that they had intended to sell a range of colors, and since the bundles were twenty-five flowers of all one color they'd have to buy at least a hundred just to get a color mix. Jesse thought they could sell more—a lot more. Peter finally suggested they try about two hundred flowers and an equal number of suckers. Everyone looked at Ben.

"Well," he said uncomfortably. "There is one little thing . . ."

"What?" Jesse asked suspiciously.

"To get the price I quoted on the suckers, we'd have to buy five hundred."

"Five hundred!" Nicole exclaimed. "You're crazy!"

"No. No, not really," Ben said hurriedly. "Five hundred times twenty cents is only a hundred dollars. And even if we don't sell them all—"

"Yeah, yeah," Nicole interrupted. "We've already heard the argument. We're not made of money, Ben, and we still have to buy the flowers."

In the end, though, they decided to go for the five hundred suckers, along with eight bundles of carnations: three red, two pink, two peppermint, and one white.

"So, let's see. That's two hundred dollars, right?" Peter asked.

"Well, plus shipping." Ben kept his eyes down on his papers. "Shipping's going to be, um . . . forty-five dollars."

"Forty-five dollars!" screeched Nicole. "Are you kidding me?"

"It's because of the flowers. They have to be shipped overnight. But there isn't any tax," Ben added defensively. "It all comes out in the wash."

"Whose wash?" Nicole demanded. "You should have figured that much shipping into all those profit estimates you did. Now we have to start over."

"No we don't." Peter finished some quick calculations on Jenna's pad. "If we sell everything at the prices we discussed, we'll collect four hundred and fifty dollars. Subtract costs and we still clear two hundred dollars. That's not bad for a couple of afternoons' work."

"Sell the suckers for seventy-five cents and you can add another hundred and twenty-five," Jesse said.

Ben glanced timidly around the room. "I really think we can sell them for a dollar. That means we'd make almost *five* hundred dollars."

"All right. I'm convinced," said Miguel. "So how much do we all put in? Thirty dollars?"

"That's good," Ben said quickly. "If everyone puts in thirty, I'll put in the extra five."

"As long as we end up with enough, it doesn't really matter who puts in what. We'll pay everybody back." Peter took out his wallet and laid a twenty and a ten on the table. "I can put in another twenty. . . ."

Everyone had brought enough of their own money, though, and soon Ben was stuffing a wad of bills into his pocket. "Okay!" he said happily. "That's it! I'll bring everything to school on Thursday."

A few minutes later, everyone but Jenna stood to go. Leah, Miguel, and Ben were first out the door, Nicole following close behind. Peter drifted toward the doorway too, while Jenna scribbled away at some final notes. Melanie maneuvered nearer the exit, hoping to catch a minute alone with him. She didn't even know what she wanted to say. It just seemed like they never talked anymore, and she missed the closer friendship they'd once had.

She should have known better than to try with Jenna around, though. Melanie had barely stepped forward, barely opened her mouth to speak, when Jenna rushed up and grabbed Peter's hand.

"All done," she said, holding up her closed steno pad. "See you at school tomorrow, Melanie," she added, pulling Peter out the door.

"Yeah. Thanks, Melanie," he called back over his shoulder.

"See you," she echoed faintly.

She turned away from the door only to come face to face with Jesse.

"I think that ship has sailed," he said smugly. "Though why you'd want to catch it still beats the heck out of me."

Melanie narrowed her eyes. "That's good. If you understood, I might have to completely revise my opinion of you."

Jesse's lip curled slightly, but he left without another word.

"He probably couldn't think of a comeback," she muttered, turning her attention to cleaning up the mess in the poolhouse.

Grabbing a trash bag, she began collecting open cans, pouring the last dregs of soda out in the sink behind the bar. At first her irritation with Jesse put some energy into her step, but it all drained away too soon, leaving her even emptier than before. She stood in the middle of the abandoned room, a half-full trash bag dangling from her fingers, feeling sick at heart.

Was this all there was to life? Being alone all the time? Fighting with the people she supposedly loved?

Melanie drew in a ragged breath as the first tears wet her cheeks. The truth was she had no idea what the purpose of life was, or if there even was one.

I only know there has to be more than this.

Five

Swallowing her pride, Nicole waited for Courtney at her locker between classes Friday morning.

"Hey, Court," she said when her friend finally appeared, trying to act as if their Wednesday fight about Emily Dooley had never happened. "Do you want me to drive us to the away game tonight? My mom let me have the car."

Courtney gave her an incredulous look, then began spinning her combination. "*Now* you want to go to the game with me? That figures."

Nicole could have passed on the basketball game, actually, but she had gone to a lot of trouble to free up her schedule that night, trading a girl named Ann for a Sunday shift instead of her usual Friday one. With Emily back in the picture, Nicole didn't want to risk making Courtney angrier by missing another game. "Of course I want to go. Don't you?"

Courtney shook her head. "Maybe if you had asked me before. But I already made plans with Emily for tonight."

Nicole clenched her teeth until they hurt. She should have guessed Emily would invite Courtney to the game—that was exactly the way the girl operated. But this wasn't seventh grade anymore, and things were going to be different. If Emily wanted to fight dirty, Nicole would beat her at her own game.

"Fine," she said, forcing a cheerful tone. "Why don't I come along too? I don't see any reason the three of us can't go together. Do you?"

Courtney slammed her locker and turned around with an armload of books. "Yeah, I do, actually. Emily and I aren't going to the game."

"Not going! When I couldn't go to the last game you acted like it was some kind of tragedy."

"Gee, Nicole, do you think that could have been because you blew me off without a reason? Besides, Em invited me to the NewBoyz concert tonight."

"NewBoyz!" cried Nicole, outmaneuvered again. "But that's all the way in Springfield! Besides, it's been sold out for months."

"And yet, Em has tickets," Courtney taunted. "Eerie, isn't it? It's almost like she *knew* this was going to happen."

She smiled before she turned and walked off down the hall. "See you around, Nicole. Maybe your buddy Jenna is holding a prayer meeting you could go to."

Nicole watched her go—half hating her, half sick at the thought of losing her friendship. She and

Courtney had been friends for so long, had been through so much together . . . but for the last few months it seemed that all they had done was fight.

We're growing apart every day, Nicole realized. *If I want to end this friendship, all I have to do is walk away and let nature and Emily take their course.*

Even the fact that she could think such a thing surprised her. She didn't want to end her friendship with Courtney.

Did she?

"Hello?" Melanie snatched up the kitchen phone before its ringing could rouse her father. She was already dressed to cheer, expecting Tanya to pick her up for the game any minute, and it would be easier if she could simply slip out unnoticed. Her eyes strained anxiously toward the front door.

"Hello," said a woman's voice. "Is this Melanie?"

"Yes. Who's this?"

"This is your aunt Gwen! I got your letter today, and I was so glad to hear from you."

"Oh." Melanie squeezed her eyes shut and almost groaned aloud.

What timing!

She was already sorry she'd ever mailed such a desperate letter. The last thing she needed was for her father to come out for another beer and catch her talking to his dead wife's sister.

"I was hoping we could get together," her aunt said, getting straight to the point. "I'd love to have you spend the weekend at my house. If you're free, I could pick you up tomorrow morning."

"Oh, no," Melanie said quickly. "I couldn't have you drive all the way out here just to pick me up. That's four hours each way." Not to mention that she had absolutely no desire to go to Iowa for the weekend. Or ever, really.

Why, why, why did I mail that stupid letter? She never should have revealed so much to a total stranger.

"I don't mind," Aunt Gwen said determinedly. "I like to drive, and I hardly ever find an excuse this good."

"Oh."

"So will you come? I'll drive you home Sunday, too, so your father isn't bothered."

Melanie almost smiled, wondering if her aunt realized how important not bothering her father was. "I don't know. . . ."

"Please?" Aunt Gwen pressed. "We're dying to see you."

The woman's obvious eagerness did nothing to allay Melanie's second thoughts, and neither did the use of the pronoun *we*. What did these people want from her? If life had taught her anything so far, it was that everyone wanted something.

A car horn sounded in the driveway. Melanie flinched, desperate to get to Tanya before another honk sent her father shuffling out in his bathrobe.

"I, uh—"

"I'll pick you up at eight. How's that? I know it's a little early, but that gives us plenty of time to get back here for a nice long lunch."

"I—"

The horn honked again, longer this time.

"Yes. All right," said Melanie, giving in. "But I have to go now."

"Fantastic! I can't wait to see you."

"Okay. Bye."

The phone was an inch off the cradle when Melanie suddenly snatched it back up, her pulse pounding double-time. "Aunt Gwen?"

"Yes?"

"Do me a favor, all right? Don't honk."

Jesse walked into the Lakehouse Lodge and stopped in the middle of the lobby, surprised by the luxury of his surroundings. He had never been to the hotel before, never even been to the back side of the lake, and he definitely wouldn't have guessed that such a nice hotel was hidden in the woods of Clearwater Crossing. Fancier than even the country club, it clearly catered to a clientele Jesse hadn't imagined vacationed in Missouri.

"Jesse!" a woman's voice cried, yanking his attention away from an enormous chandelier. "Jesse, there you are!"

His mother was rushing toward him across the parquet floor, her arms open wide. A moment later he was in them, hugging her fiercely.

"You've gotten taller," she said at last. A trace of tears glistened in her eyes as she dropped her arms. "It's been too long since I've seen you. You're practically all grown up!"

Jesse shrugged, embarrassed. "You look different too."

"Different how?"

But he couldn't put his finger on it. There had been no major changes—her light brown hair was still shoulder length, her eyes were as blue, her tan as healthy. She simply seemed altered in the little, indefinable ways that people change when they're no longer seen every day, or even every month.

"I don't know," he admitted. "It's just been a long time."

She nodded and smoothed the lapels of her gray silk jacket. "Well, we'll have to make sure not to let so much time pass again."

"I wanted to fly out for Christmas," he reminded her.

"I know." A shadow crossed her face. "Let's not talk about that now."

Shaking off the memory, she grabbed him by one hand. "They have the cutest restaurant here," she said, pulling him through the lobby. "Since there wasn't anywhere special you wanted to eat, I went ahead and made us a reservation."

"All right," he said, distracted by a wall of glass opening onto the lake behind the hotel. The water gleamed like a mirror in the twilight, but all that struck Jesse was how freezing it must be. February in the Ozarks might be mild by Midwest standards, but it was still brutal compared to what he'd been used to back home. Sure, the sun came out every once in a while, but it didn't do much good. He was starting to believe his toes would never be warm again.

The restaurant his mother led him to had hunting-lodge decor, with duck decoys sprouting flower arrangements and light fixtures made from deer antlers. The maitre d' showed them to a red-draped table by a window and handed them leather-bound menus.

"Order anything you like," Jesse's mother urged, beaming. "My treat."

But as he scanned the sky-high prices, Jesse heard his father's words as if the man were there: "It's easy for her to be generous—I'm paying." And in that moment, Jesse almost hated him for making money an issue on top of everything else.

Wasn't it enough that their family had been torn apart? That Jesse had been dragged halfway across the country to live with a woman he hated? Wasn't it enough that his real mother seemed almost a stranger now as she smiled at him across the table? So much damage had already been done by his parents' divorce—did he really need to feel guilty about the alimony too?

The waiter came, ready to take their order.

"I'll have the lobster," Jesse announced recklessly. "*And* the prime rib."

His mother laughed. "You'd better bring a side of doggy bags with that," she jokingly told the waiter.

"Don't worry, I'll eat it," Jesse said determinedly. "Do you have a dessert cart here?" he asked the waiter. "Cheesecake? Crème brûlée?"

"Both," the man said, nodding. "Plus a chocolate-raspberry torte to die for. You might want to take a look before you make your final decision."

Jesse shook his head. "Just save a plate with all three."

"It must be wonderful to have a teenage boy's metabolism," his mother sighed as the waiter went off for their salads. "I've never been able to eat like that in my life."

"I don't do it very often. Just on special occasions."

He only wished there was some way he could add an expensive bottle of wine to the bill. He knew his mother wouldn't let him drink it, but he'd have really loved telling his father that the two of them had dropped a couple of hundred dollars on dinner.

Oh well, he thought. *I'll just have to do my best to make it up in food.*

All through the meal, he and his mother tried to find their old rhythm, to pick up where they'd left off, but they couldn't quite hit their old stride. The conversation was pleasant enough—she asked about his school and friends, he asked about his brothers—but there was no real sense of connection. All the things they *weren't* saying lurked right beneath the surface, making everything else seem like whitewash.

On top of that, Jesse couldn't stop thinking about how different his mother looked. He hadn't lain eyes on her since the couple of midsummer weeks he'd spent visiting in California, and now it seemed he had to relearn her features. He imagined her doing the same for him, knowing he'd probably changed more than she had, and wondered if the differences made her sad too.

"Well, I didn't believe you could do it, but I was wrong," she teased as he forced the last bite of dessert into his mouth.

From what he could still taste, Jesse was willing to believe the chocolate-raspberry torte was as good as the waiter had said, but it definitely lost appeal as the third dessert after two enormous dinners.

"Everything was great," he said, making himself swallow. He felt kind of sick to his stomach, but he wasn't about to admit it.

"So what should we do tomorrow? Do you want me to come by and pick you up, or do you want to meet me here?"

"I'll meet you here," he said quickly. He didn't even want to contemplate the possibility of his mom and Elsa ending up in the same room. Or his mom and dad either, for that matter.

"All right. Maybe that's best."

They discussed breakfast plans, even though Jesse was sure he would never eat again. His mother thought she might like to go hiking around the lake.

"You don't see trees like this in Malibu," she said. "I'm glad I brought my walking shoes."

"Did you bring your ski clothes? That's more important."

"Don't be such a wet blanket. It's beautiful outside!"

"Wait," he advised sourly. "Tomorrow you could wake up to snow, sun, hail . . . it's anybody's guess. The weather here isn't like home at all."

His mother looked at him strangely. "Don't you think of *this* as your home now?"

"Yeah!" Jesse snorted. "Good one."

He was still thinking about that exchange as he pulled his car into the Joneses' garage later that night. Did his mother really believe he was *happy* in Clearwater Crossing?

His father and Elsa accosted him in the entry before he could escape up the stairs to his room.

"A little late, aren't you?" his father asked, tapping the watch on his wrist. "I thought you were just having dinner."

"That must have been a pretty big dinner," Elsa said sarcastically, hovering behind her husband.

"You have no idea." Jesse put one hand on the stair rail, ready to escape. "And I'm tired now, sooo . . ."

"I'm not surprised," said Elsa, "after you spent the whole day at school. I don't know why she couldn't just see you tomorrow. She's going to be here all week."

And I don't know what business it is of yours, Jesse longed to tell her, sick of her catty remarks. "That hardly makes up for the rest of the year," he said instead, his eyes daring her to push it further.

Amazingly, she didn't, and neither did his father.

"We'll see you tomorrow, then," Dr. Jones said.

Not if I see you first, Jesse thought.

Halfway up the stairs, he nearly tripped over Brittany crouched at the turn on the landing.

"What are you doing?" he snarled. "Were you spying on me?"

"No!" she said, jumping up. "No, Jesse, I—"

"Get a life, you pathetic snoop!"

"I heard that!" Elsa warned from below.

Good, because that goes double for you!

"Okay," Caitlin murmured into the telephone, her cheeks flushed scarlet. "Okay, you too. Bye."

She pressed the Disconnect button and turned her

back on Jenna, setting the phone on the ledge behind their beds.

"So?" Jenna prompted, nearly dying of curiosity. She knew her sister had been talking to David, but trying to make sense of a conversation from just Caitlin's end was harder than working a jigsaw puzzle without the box top. "For Pete's sake, Caitlin, what did he say?"

Caitlin finally twisted back around, a smile all over her face. "He's coming to town next weekend. We have a date for Valentine's Day."

"Yes!" Jenna screamed, leaping off her bed and throwing both fists in the air. "Caitlin, that's fantastic!"

Caitlin stayed on her bed, her face turning even redder. "I'm happy, of course, but I'm really nervous, too."

Jenna dropped down beside her and grabbed both her sister's hands. "Nervous? No. You're just *excited*."

"Well, sure I'm excited. But, Jenna . . . this is my first date."

It's true, Jenna realized. Shy Caitlin had been a total recluse in high school, never going to even a single dance. The only events she'd attended were ones Mary Beth had dragged her to: a few games, some pep rallies—that was about it.

"You and David did go to brunch," Jenna reminded her.

"Yes, but that wasn't really a date. I mean, we were just talking and David said he hadn't eaten yet and the next thing I knew we were in the car on the way to the restaurant. If I'd known we were going beforehand, I'd have been a total wreck."

Jenna nodded, not seeing any point in denying the obvious. "So tell me about Valentine's Day! Where are you two going?"

"Out to dinner somewhere. I'm not sure where."

"What are you going to wear?"

Caitlin shook her head. "I don't know. You and Peter are going out to dinner too, right? What are you going to wear?"

"Hey, you know what?" Jenna said, getting a great idea. "We ought to go shopping together! We'll both get new outfits, and presents for the guys."

"It's a little early to be giving David presents, don't you think? I don't even know what I'd get him."

"Something small, or even just a card," Jenna suggested, already lost in the more interesting question of what she'd get for Peter. "So should we go? I'll ask Mom for the car."

Caitlin shook her head, pointing to the clock. "The stores will be closed by the time we get there. We could go tomorrow, though."

"Oh. All right." It was kind of a letdown not to leave right that minute, but Saturday would be better. They could take their time and really make a day of it, maybe have lunch at the mall. . . .

"It's a date," said Jenna.

Caitlin turned scarlet again. "I know. I can't believe it."

Jenna didn't bother to explain what she'd really meant. Instead she dropped belly-down on her bed, her chin in her hands and her head full of dreams about her first Valentine's Day as Peter's girlfriend. Everything was going to be so perfect! She imagined the dress she would buy, and Peter's face when he opened her gift.

And there was the even more intriguing question of what Peter would give her. . . .

"This is going to be the best Valentine's Day ever!" she burst out excitedly, turning to her sister.

Caitlin smiled. "You won't get any argument from me."

Six

"You'll have to come back in a couple of months," Aunt Gwen said as she and Melanie picked their way through the snow between the carport and the front of her house. "Everything's prettier when the trees are green and the flowers are blooming. Now it's all just white."

Melanie didn't reply as she followed her aunt to the door of a one-story, white-shingled cottage. The weather in southern Iowa was harsher than in Clearwater Crossing, and snow coated everything. The trees and ground were white, and so was the picket fence around the little square of yard out front. The porch was painted white as well, the dark green front door and two outdoor chairs making the only spots of color. Melanie gripped her luggage a little tighter, sure her aunt was right about things looking better in the spring. She was equally sure, however, that she wouldn't be back to check them out. By then she'd already have seen what she'd come to see, so what would be the point?

"And of course you'll want to visit with your

grandparents," Aunt Gwen continued. "It's such a shame I didn't know they were leaving town this weekend. I wanted to surprise them with your visit and, well . . . sometimes surprises backfire, I guess."

"Hmm," said Melanie, hoping her relief didn't show in her face. Her mother had barely spoken to her parents for years before her death, and knowing that didn't make Melanie eager to see them. In fact, finding out she wouldn't have to had been the best news she'd heard so far.

"And I'm sorry about all those interruptions during lunch," Aunt Gwen apologized as she unlocked the front door. "Small-town curiosity, you know? And you *do* look so much like your mother."

"Right."

If Melanie hadn't known that before, she couldn't doubt it now. It seemed everyone in town—or at least everyone who ate at the restaurant they'd gone to for lunch—knew Aunt Gwen, and most seemed to remember Melanie's mother, Tristyn, too. People kept making excuses to stop by their table and talk to Gwen, but Melanie knew she was the one on display. She could barely keep the smile on her face after the fourth or fifth time. Aunt Gwen's friends seemed nice enough, but it was still painful pretending to eat while making small talk with total strangers.

Not that the four-hour car ride to Iowa from Clearwater Crossing had been particularly relaxing.

Or that Aunt Gwen was much more than a stranger herself.

Her aunt had shown up promptly at eight, and Melanie had snuck out to meet her in the driveway. Restricting her luggage to a backpack and a tote bag, just in case her father glanced out, she'd left him a note that said she was spending the weekend with a girlfriend. When she'd caught her first look at Aunt Gwen, however, she'd almost changed her mind.

Gwen bore almost no resemblance to her only sister. Whereas Tristyn had been a green-eyed blonde, Gwen's hair was brown, her eyes a grayish sort of blue. But Melanie was still shaken by the jolt of recognition as her gaze met her aunt's through the windshield. She and Aunt Gwen had never been close, and Melanie hadn't seen her in over two years. Even so, Gwen's face seemed hauntingly familiar. As she'd jumped out of the car, even the facts that she was leaner than Melanie had remembered and that there were new streaks of gray at her temples hadn't erased the eerie sense that they were somehow picking up their relationship exactly where they'd left off. Except that they'd never *had* a relationship. . . .

Melanie's hands had shaken as she'd handed over her bags. And despite every attempt Gwen had made to put her at ease since then, she had never been more on her guard.

"Well, this is it," her aunt said now, flipping a light switch by the door. "Home sweet home."

Gwen's whole house looked nearly small enough to fit inside Melanie's living room, but the open floor plan and high ceilings made it cozy rather than cramped. Spotlights shone down from the beams overhead, giving the impression of a sunny day despite the gray skies outside. Potted ferns filled the corners and ivy cascaded from one end of a kitchen counter lined with bar stools. The wooden floors were dotted with pastel throw rugs; the furniture was primarily overstuffed wicker.

"It's cute," Melanie said uncertainly, still holding on to her bags. The style was so different from that of her own house, the house her mother had designed. Shouldn't sisters have more in common?

"Thanks." Aunt Gwen strode through the main room toward an open doorway across from the kitchen. "Come on, I'll show you where you're bunking. You do like cats, right?"

"I guess. I've never had one."

Her aunt stopped short, turning around with an astonished look on her face. "Are you kidding me? Never?"

"Well . . . it's not like I'm a hundred."

Gwen laughed. "No. I suppose you still have time."

Inside the small guest room, an enormous gray cat glared from the center of a thick white comforter.

"Meet Max," said her aunt. "This is his bed, but I'm sure the two of you will work something out."

"Hello, Max." Melanie dropped her bags and stretched out her hand to him.

Max drew back, his yellow eyes huge. His ruff stood out like a lion's mane, doubling in size.

"You be nice," Aunt Gwen reproached him, "or I'll make you sleep outside."

Max stared balefully, then leapt off the bed and fled.

"I don't think he likes me," Melanie said.

"He'll warm up. Right now he's just appalled by the suggestion that an animal could sleep outside."

"You wouldn't really make him, right? I mean, it *is* pretty cold."

Gwen smiled—Melanie's mother's smile. "Not a chance. You know what they say about single women and their cats, and I'm afraid in my case it's all true. Max is so spoiled he thinks cold is what happens when I open the refrigerator."

She looked around the guest room, then twitched a white curtain open. "I hope you'll be comfortable here. I know it's small, but there's space in the closet if you want to hang anything, and the top two drawers are empty."

There was a lamp on the tall, narrow dresser Gwen pointed to. That and the single bed were the only furniture in the room.

"It's fine," said Melanie, trying not to compare its size to her walk-in closet at home.

"All right, then. Make yourself comfortable. I'm

just going to use the bathroom, and put out some towels for you. Do you like yellow?"

"Yellow's fine."

"Because I have purple too."

"Either one. It doesn't matter."

"I'll surprise you, then."

Her aunt finally withdrew, leaving Melanie alone in the room.

For a moment she stood looking around her, lost and ill at ease. Then she lifted her tote bag onto the bed and hung up a couple of things. Since she was only staying overnight, she hadn't brought much, but rattling the hangers gave her something to do. Max stalked back in as she closed the closet door, leaping onto the center of the bed and staring her down as if daring her to object.

"You can have it," Melanie told him, sidling out the door. "You don't need all that attitude for me."

She wandered around the main room, trying to get her bearings. On a ledge above the dining nook, she found a collection of framed photographs. She supposed they were all family pictures, but she barely noticed the others as her eyes went straight to the one in the center. It was a picture of her—except that it wasn't.

"Oh my God," she whispered. "I *do* look like my mom."

Her own face smiled out at her, side by side with a face she recognized as that of a much younger Gwen.

The two teenagers stood beside a moss-green swimming hole, dressed in tank tops and shorts, their arms looped around each other.

"Those were good times," her aunt said behind her, jolting Melanie back to Earth with a start. "The pond's still a great place to swim, and the last time I was there the kids had rigged a rope swing to that tree. They were swinging out over the water, splashing down like hippopotami. Is that a word? Hippopotamuses, maybe. Either way, it looked like a lot of fun. You'll have to come back here this summer and try it."

"Uh-huh," Melanie said vacantly, her eyes still on the photograph. Seeing her mother so young, so happy, so *alive* amazed her so much that she didn't even remember she wasn't coming back.

"Are you *sure* this is safe, Benny?" Mrs. Pipkin asked, leaning over her son's shoulder to peer suspiciously at the computer monitor. "I've heard all kinds of stories about Internet thieves who get your credit-card number and—"

"Yes, it's safe!" Ben insisted. "This is a totally secure site. How many times do I have to tell you?"

"Don't get smart with me," his mother warned. "I don't have to let you use my credit card at all."

"I know. But Mom, you've got to trust me. I know what I'm doing here."

"So you say," she replied skeptically, stalking out

of the den, where Ben had logged on to his father's computer.

Ben waited until he was sure she was out of hearing. "What a worrier," he muttered, returning to his task.

There was absolutely no reason to be paranoid about doing business online. Everybody did it—even computer novices. And Ben was certainly no novice. As he finished checking his item numbers and scrolled down to the onscreen order blank, he had never felt more on top of his game.

"Nothing to it," he congratulated himself, scanning the incredibly simple form. "This couldn't be easier."

All he had to do was fill in his name and address, then indicate the item numbers and the desired quantity of each in the little boxes provided. The computer took care of everything else, automatically inserting the prices and delivery charges and totaling the order.

"Okay, first the suckers," Ben said, entering the item number he had copied previously and a quantity of five hundred. The subtotal box immediately showed one hundred dollars, exactly as expected. "Cool."

With a pleased smile on his face, Ben set about ordering the eight bundles of carnations—three red, two pink, two peppermint, and one white—exactly as agreed upon by Eight Prime. Each color had a different item number, and Ben took his time checking and rechecking until he was sure he had his order exactly right before he directed the program to add the delivery charge for shipping everything to his doorstep. Finally he typed in his mother's credit-card number and scrolled down to the Send button that would submit his order via e-mail.

But just as he was about to click it, he noticed more writing below.

"What's all this?" he muttered, scrolling lower and starting to read out loud. "To fill in the name field, type your name or the name of your company in the space provided. You may use upper- and lowercase letters, or all capitals. If you use a company name, type it exactly as shown on your company check in the space provided for *first or company name*. If you use a personal name, put the last and first names in the separate spaces provided for *last* and *first* names, respectively. If you—"

Ben broke off reading. "What do they think?" he scoffed. "That I'm a complete idiot?"

He couldn't imagine that anyone with enough on the ball to log on to a computer and find an online store could be so pathetically in need of guidance when it came to filling out a simple form. Still, judging by the painfully detailed instructions for entering a delivery address, that was exactly what this company thought. Ben scrolled down a little farther, scanning impatiently.

"Please!" he exclaimed a second later. "I feel sorry for anyone who needs this much help."

Scrolling back up without reading the rest, he clicked the Send button with total confidence, pleased with his morning's work.

Just wait until Eight Prime sees what I bought, he thought happily. *Between the prices I got and how easy it was, they're all going to be way impressed!*

Nicole carried her tray of nearly empty ketchup and mustard dispensers carefully from the Wienerageous dining room to the kitchen. The restaurant had been packed from the moment she'd arrived that Saturday and, stuck on dining room duty once more, she'd already gone through her backup tray of condiments. She successfully negotiated the gate in the counter, then skirted the end of the pass-through wall into the kitchen.

"If it isn't the Queen of Ketchup," Ajax greeted her. His sarcasm lacked a little of its usual glee, however, and sweat ran down both sides of his face. His spatula hovered over a grill loaded with burgers while his fellow cook, Eric, prepped buns at top speed, barely able to keep up with the orders being shouted back from the registers.

"What does that make you?" Nicole asked irritably. "The Minister of Meat?"

Eric howled with laughter, but Ajax didn't seem to mind in the slightest.

"I like it!" he said, puffing up.

"You would."

Before he could make any further wisecracks, Nicole walked to the back of the kitchen and set her tray on a section of countertop outside the walk-in refrigerator, where Gail was chopping onions.

"Enjoying yourself?" Gail asked dryly as Nicole pulled a giant plastic jar of mustard out of cold storage and began looking around for the funnel.

"Yeah, sure. It looks like you're having even more fun, though. Why don't we just get a food processor?"

Gail shook her head. "Why don't we buy our onions already chopped, like the rest of the fast-food world? They come in big milk-carton things, you know."

"Are you kidding me?"

"Not about this."

Nicole glanced back over her shoulder. Eric and Ajax were still hustling out orders, and the last time she'd seen Mr. Roarke he'd been filling out paperwork in the break room. For the moment, no one was watching the girls.

"Help me find the ketchup," Nicole said suddenly, grabbing her cousin by the sleeve.

Gail barely managed to set down her butcher knife before being pulled into the giant steel refrigerator. Nicole tugged the heavy door nearly shut behind them.

"This is the pits!" she complained, referring to the day's work assignments. "I can't believe I'm back in the dining room."

"What did you expect? You're still the newest employee."

"Yes, but last week I was on counter."

Gail looked at her disbelievingly. "Wake up, Nicole! Last week I was on register. It'll probably be a good long time before either of us works the counter again."

"But why? I thought you were going out with him again last night."

Gail shot a nervous look at the door Nicole had left cracked open, then grabbed the interior handle and pulled it closed completely. The big cooler was now a sealed vault lined with wire shelves full of cheese and pickles. "I did. Don't remind me."

"Then what's his problem?" whined Nicole. "Didn't things go well?"

"Did you think they could?" Gail asked incredulously.

"Well . . ." Nicole hadn't devoted a lot of time to thinking about it, actually, preferring to dwell on more pleasant subjects. "It couldn't have been any more awful than last time."

"That's what you think," Gail said darkly. "You're not the one he's trying to seduce."

Thank heavens! thought Nicole, not sure if the

goose bumps that suddenly erupted on her arms were from the freezing temperature in the cooler or the sheer horror of such a thought. She rubbed them down with both hands, trying not to let her disgust show on her face.

"Well, but so . . .you still didn't let him kiss you or anything. Did you?"

Gail grimaced. "I couldn't avoid it. I mean, this time he just came right out and said, 'I'm going to kiss you. Don't duck.' What was I going to do?"

Nicole was too revolted even to consider the possibilities. "Oh, Gail!"

"Pretty gross, huh? But not as gross as when he told me that dating implies 'certain things.' "

Nicole felt the bile rise in her throat. "He didn't! Ugh! I mean . . . what exactly did he mean?"

Gail made a face. "I think it's pretty obvious. Believe me, though, I didn't ask for details."

Nicole only stared, her mind reeling. When Mr. Roarke had first asked Gail to go out with him, his request had seemed unpleasant, maybe even a little pathetic, but nothing worse than that. Nicole had never dreamed that he would try to take things any further than dinner or a movie. After all, he was an adult, and Gail was just . . .

"Gail, this is bad," she blurted out. "I mean, this is *really* bad. You're not going out with him again."

Gail didn't say anything.

"Right?" Nicole insisted, upset.

"I have to. But don't worry—it's not like he's going to force me into anything. I can take care of Mr. Roarke."

"You say that, but—"

"But what? Give it a rest, Nicole. You're the one who wanted me to go out with him in the first place."

"Yes, but I never thought . . ." Nicole trailed off, confused. What hadn't she thought? That things would go this far? That the punishment might be worse than the crime?

The truth was, she just hadn't thought. At least, not any further than saving her own skin.

Because this was *Gail's fault,* she reminded herself defensively. *I just wanted her to take care of the mess she made. But I never—*

"Look, don't worry about it, Nicole," said her cousin, an easy smile on her face. "I've got everything under control."

"Are you sure? Because it doesn't sound under control. Maybe . . . maybe we ought to tell our parents."

"*Now?* Are you crazy? I didn't go this far just to give up when this thing is almost over. Besides, I thought you were so scared of getting fired."

Nicole *was* scared, and she knew Gail must be too. "Well . . . if you're *sure* you have it under control."

"A lot more under control than it'll be if Mr.

85

Roarke catches us gabbing in the freezer. Come on. Relax!"

With a friendly push on Nicole's shoulder, Gail exited through the heavy steel door, leaving her alone. Nicole stared after her a moment, then abruptly began looking for the ketchup.

If Gail's okay with this, then why should I worry? she asked herself, desperate to ease her suddenly guilty conscience. *After all, it's not like I forced her into dating him. And I'm certainly not the one who got her into trouble in the first place.*

Nicole found the ketchup but didn't leave the freezer. *In fact, I tried to straighten her out.*

You didn't try very hard, her conscience nagged. *You could have reported her behavior to someone before Mr. Roarke caught her red-handed. Or—after he did— you could have encouraged her to take her punishment instead of dating him. At least if we'd been fired, this would all be over.*

Sort of, she amended, wincing at the thought of what her parents would have done if she'd been fired. Shuddering involuntarily, she clutched the cold tub of ketchup to her chest. Anything had to be better than having their parents find out.

Didn't it?

Gail's got things under control, Nicole reassured herself, taking a deep, calming breath. *If she's not worrying, why should I?*

* * *

Jesse picked up a rock and threw it over the edge of the bluff he and his mother had hiked to. It hit something soft down below—an unmelted pocket of snow or a pile of sodden leaves—disappearing without a sound.

"What's down there?" his mother asked, peering over the edge.

"More of the same," he said. "Trees. Rocks. The usual."

His mother laughed. "We'll have to call you Nature Boy. I can see how much you appreciate it."

"I *do* appreciate it. I appreciate surf and sand. But out here everything's just wet or freezing. Except in the summer. In summertime, the air gets so hot it's like a weight pressing down on your shoulders. I hate it here."

"It *is* a little cold today." But though his mother's tone was light, her eyes searched his face. "Maybe we should head back to the lodge."

"With pleasure!" Jesse agreed, turning to walk toward the hotel.

They'd been wandering through the woods around the lake for hours. At first he hadn't minded, but as the afternoon had worn on and he'd grown colder and more uncomfortable, the problems of the last few weeks had begun preying on his mind to the point where he could barely think about anything else. Between the breakup with Melanie, his deteriorating relationship with his father, and the constant irritation of living with Brittany and Elsa, Jesse had grown more and more sullen, worrying about everything that was wrong with his life. Even the fact that he was finally spending time with his mother, something he knew he ought to be glad about, hadn't broken his gloom. If anything, her presence had only added to his bad mood, another reminder that life wasn't what it should be.

"Oh, look at that pretty tree!" she said, pointing somewhere off the path.

"Uh-huh," he replied without turning his head.

"You know, Steve is really enjoying the botany class he's taking at college this semester. He sent me a card on some paper he made himself, with pretty leaves pressed into it."

"Steve always did like to make stuff."

"Yes, but both your brothers are really blossoming at college. They seem so happy there."

"Why *wouldn't* they be happy?" Jesse asked bitterly. "They're free."

When his parents had finally begun divorce proceedings, it had been during the summer between Jesse's eighth- and ninth-grade years. His oldest brother, Kevin, had already completed a year at MIT and hadn't even come home that summer, no doubt to avoid the constant fighting. Steven was about to start his senior year of high school and should have been around. Instead he had lasted barely a month before he'd moved in with a friend, ultimately taking early graduation and leaving for Princeton a semester before he could start. Only Jesse had had to hang around through all the wrangling—and sometimes it was hard not to hate his brothers for deserting him.

That hadn't been the worst part, though. The worst had been learning that his mother had given his father custody of him, despite the fact that the traitor had already announced his intention of marrying Elsa. Jesse had protested, but his mother stood firm.

"A teenage boy needs his father," she'd said. "Besides, you'll be better off. I don't even know where I'll live once this house sells, and it won't be long before you're off to college. I don't want to give your father any excuse not to pay for your education. Believe me, it's for the best. I'm only thinking of you."

Of course, neither one of them had imagined Dr. Jones would ever leave Malibu, not to mention California. . . .

"Jesse, are you really that unhappy here?" his mother asked now from behind him on the trail. Her hand grabbed the back of his jacket, stopping his progress.

He turned, amazed to see her eyes brimming with tears.

"I wanted to do the right thing. Your father and I . . . that hadn't been good for years. I held on as long as I could."

"Really? Seems like you bailed and made me live with him."

"I honestly thought it was best. Your father and I were a disaster together, but he loves you boys. He's always been a good father."

"He *used* to be a good father. Now all he thinks about is himself and Elsa and whatever it is we're doing in this backwater town. I do hate it here. I hate everything about this place!"

His voice had risen to a shout, and unshed tears stung his eyes, but Jesse had said too much to back down. "I never even hear from you, or Steve or Kevin. I feel like the Lone Ranger."

His mother pushed back her hair, her hand resting on top of her head. "But you must have friends, Jesse. You had so many at home."

"Yes, and I *miss* them! I know people here, but there's no one I'd be sorry to leave." He closed his mind, refusing to think of Melanie. "I wish I could go back and live with you in California."

The words were out before he could stop them. He knew she'd say no, the way she always had before.

But his mother didn't answer right away. Instead she kept her gaze on the ground, dragging the toe of her hiking boot over the muddy path. When her eyes finally met his again, she didn't make any attempt to hide the way they were spilling over.

"I don't want to say anything right now," she

floored him by announcing. "We have a week; let's think it over."

"Are you serious? You're not just saying no?"

"I'm not saying yes, either. All I'm saying is, I miss you all the time. And if you're so unhappy here, and I'm unhappy too . . . well, maybe we can find a way to make things better for both of us."

A cold wind gusted across the trail, but Jesse barely felt it. Mentally, he was back on the beach, breathing the warm salt air. His old life shimmered before his eyes, even more attractive than when he'd left it. To turn back the clock, to forget everything that had happened to him over the past year in Missouri . . .

In his mind, he was already packing.

Seven

"Are you sure you want to do this?" Caitlin asked, pulling on a second, thicker pair of socks. "I mean, I appreciate the offer, but it's cold out there, and I don't really need the help."

Jenna peered through their third-story window at the slowly lightening dawn outside. There had been another freeze overnight, and her breath fogged the pane instantly. Her still unmade bed, on the other hand, looked warm and incredibly inviting. If she *didn't* help Caitlin walk dogs that Sunday, she could go back to sleep for a couple more hours. . . .

But she'd been looking forward to spending the time with her sister, chatting about the shopping they'd done the day before and their upcoming Valentine's dates. If she didn't talk to her now, before church, it was hard to say when they'd get another chance to spend some time alone together.

"No, I want to go with you," Jenna said determinedly, shedding her quilted bathrobe. "It'll be fun."

Caitlin smiled. "If you say so. But on mornings like this it's pretty easy to see why people pay me to walk their dogs."

Jenna refused to consider the truth of that statement as she went to her dresser and began digging for long underwear. She was just pulling on her pants when Sarah burst into the room, already fully dressed for the cold at an hour when everyone but Caitlin was usually still asleep.

"Are you guys walking the dogs?" she asked. "I want to go too."

"It's awfully cold out there, Sarah," Caitlin said doubtfully. "I don't think you want to come with us."

"Yes, I do," Sarah insisted, sitting on Caitlin's bed. "It's boring here. There's nothing's happening."

"Maybe because it's still barely light outside," Jenna said. "Why don't you go back to bed?"

"I'm not tired." Sarah crossed her arms with unusual stubbornness.

"Watch cartoons, then. You can have the TV in the den all to yourself."

Sarah shot her a disbelieving look. "I'm ten now, Jenna, not five."

"Maggie and Allison still watch cartoons, and they're older than you are."

"I don't want to watch cartoons. I want to walk dogs."

"Well, you can't come with us," said Jenna.

"You're too little. Those big dogs would pull you right over onto your face."

"I can hold on," Sarah insisted.

"No you can't. *I* can barely hold on to some of those dogs."

The two girls faced off, equally determined.

"She doesn't have to actually walk a dog," Caitlin said into the silence between them. "She could just tag along for the company."

"Yeah!" said Sarah.

But Caitlin had unwittingly hit on the real reason Jenna didn't want her youngest sister to go. With Sarah along, they wouldn't be able to talk about anything good. It would be all fifth grade, and class projects, and little-girl cliques.

"Look, Sarah, I want to do this with Caitlin. Mom will be happier if you stay at home anyway."

"You guys always do everything together, and no one does anything with me," Sarah pouted, jerking to her feet. "It's not fair."

"Why don't you go play with Maggie and Allison?" Jenna suggested. "They're more your age."

"I don't *want* to play with them!" Sarah nearly shouted. "They never want me around either."

"Then call a friend, or read a book," Jenna said impatiently. "For Pete's sake, Sarah, stop making this *my* problem."

Sarah rarely cried, but the look she gave Jenna as she left the room was very close to tears.

"You could have let her tag along," Caitlin said. "She wouldn't have been any trouble."

"It's not that I thought she'd be *trouble*," Jenna explained, feeling a pang of guilt. "We just wouldn't have been able to talk with her there."

"Why not?"

"Because Sarah would just want to talk about school, and her teacher, and the kids in her class. You know, little-girl stuff."

"And we want to talk about . . . ?" Caitlin prompted.

"Valentine's Day, of course! It won't be any fun gossiping about David and Peter with Sarah listening in."

Caitlin blushed a little. "Well, no. I guess not."

"We'll do something with Sarah another time," Jenna said, as much to ease her own conscience as to reassure Caitlin. "But she is only ten. She can't expect to march in here and call the shots."

"Maybe you're right," Caitlin said uncertainly.

"Of course I'm right!" said Jenna, relieved. "By the time we get back to the house, she'll have forgotten all about it."

Melanie folded a shirt and placed it on top of the other things already in her tote bag. The morning was still new—Aunt Gwen wasn't even up yet—but the drive back to Clearwater Crossing was long, and Melanie had already seen what she'd come to see.

I just want to go home, she thought, exchanging evil looks with Max. The cat had terrorized her all night, insisting on sleeping right in the middle of the bed and raising a ruckus every time she tried to move him to one side or the other. His yellow eyes glared at her now from the vantage point of the pillows.

"I won't miss you, either," she muttered, imagining him wishing her gone.

The day before had been one of the most exhausting of her life. Sitting in the car for the four-hour ride to Iowa, sitting in a restaurant for lunch, sitting in Aunt Gwen's living room shooting the breeze, sitting in the car again for a tour of the snowy sights of town, sitting down to a quiet dinner with Aunt Gwen—none of that sounded strenuous, but it had completely worn her out. The stress of being both constantly on display and constantly on guard had sent her to bed at eight-thirty, complaining of a headache.

Between the jockeying for position with Max and all the new thoughts running through her head, though, she hadn't been able to sleep. Instead she'd lain awake for hours, trying to make some sense out of the confusion in her mind.

She liked Aunt Gwen. She liked her more than she'd expected to. But that only made the rift between Gwen and Melanie's mother more inexplicable. And what about her grandparents leaving town so unexpectedly? They were old and the weather was lousy. Where could they have to go? Couldn't they have postponed? Melanie half suspected that they *were* in town and just didn't want to see her—which was fine. But then why did Aunt Gwen keep insisting they did?

"I can't believe you're up," Gwen said from the bedroom doorway, startling Melanie back to the present. "Are you always such an early riser?"

Melanie spun around, pulling her tote bag off the bed. "Uh, not really. But it's a long drive back, and I know you have to drive both ways. I thought it was better to get ready."

Her aunt waved one hand, as if to dismiss her concerns. She was wearing a thick pink bathrobe, a strip of flannel nightgown peeking out beneath its hem.

"Yesterday was the crunch day," she said, referring to the fact that she'd left at four in the morning to collect Melanie. "Today we can take our time. I thought I'd make some omelets, then after church we can think about hitting the road."

Melanie felt her eyebrows rise. "You, uh—you don't expect *me* to go to church," she said, dropping her tote bag against the bed. "I didn't even know you went."

"Oh," said Aunt Gwen. "Well, yes. I guess that might seem strange to you. I know your mother . . ." She trailed off, clearly taken aback. "You *never* go to church?"

"Never."

"Oh. Well . . . let's just have breakfast. I guess I can skip church today."

"If you want to go, don't miss it because of me."

"I can't leave you here all alone. You'd be bored."

Melanie smiled, wondering if her aunt had any idea how often she entertained herself. "I'll find something to do."

"Really?"

"Sure. It's only for an hour."

They moved to the kitchen, where Melanie took a seat on one of the barstools, watching across the counter as Gwen put a pan on the stove and broke eggs into a bowl.

"So! It looks like it's going to be sunny today," Gwen said cheerfully, changing the subject.

Melanie was happy to let her, and all through breakfast the pair exchanged similar small talk. As soon as the dishes were done, Gwen dressed for the early service.

"Are you sure you'll be okay all by yourself?" she asked, hesitating by the front door.

"No problem," Melanie told her. "I'm pretty good at that."

But after her aunt had driven away, Melanie couldn't suppress the restlessness that suddenly overcame her. She double-checked the bathroom to make sure she hadn't forgotten her toothbrush, then wandered around the main room, looking at photographs, flipping through magazines, and peering out the windows at the glittering snow outside.

I'll take a walk, she decided. It might be fun to crunch through the ice awhile, and it wouldn't hurt to kill some energy before the long car trip home. Grabbing her coat off a hook by the door, she let herself onto the porch.

Outside, the chill in the air nearly took her breath away. It had been cold the day before, too, but she hadn't arrived in town until much later. For a moment, she considered going back inside and forgetting the whole idea. But a minute later she ran down the snowy front path, swinging her leg over the low wooden fence rather than trying to open the snowed-in gate.

She had barely left her aunt's yard when a teenage girl ran out of the cottage next door, charging down to meet Melanie on the road.

"Hi!" she called, waving as she jumped her own matching gate. "Hi, I'm Kathy Kelly."

She was already pink-cheeked from the cold, and her breath made little puffs of steam as she rushed forward. Short blond hair fringed the folded brim of her rainbow-striped cap, and the bright colors in conjunction with the freckles sprinkled across her small nose made her seem like the ghost of summer in the middle of all that snow. Melanie liked her on sight.

"Hello. I'm Melanie."

"Yeah, I know. I saw you with your aunt yesterday. I was hoping I'd get to meet you."

"I was just going to walk." Melanie pointed down the road. "Do you want to . . . ?"

"Sure. Absolutely." The pom-pom on Kathy's cap bobbed with the energy of her nod. "There's a creek with a footbridge a few blocks from here. If you want, I'll show you where."

"Okay."

Melanie began to walk, relieved simply to be with someone her own age, especially since that person was a total stranger. All of her secrets were intact again. No one was digging into her past, or comparing her to her mother. . . .

Until Kathy's next words knocked her sideways.

"You know, my mom and your mom were best friends once. Mom says it's almost scary how much alike you look."

"Are you kidding me?"

"No. She says you're dead ringers."

That wasn't the part Melanie had questioned. "What's your mom's name?"

"Lisa. Lisa Kelly."

Melanie had never heard of her. Then again, there were so many things she didn't know about her mother.

"I sure wish you were moving in," Kathy said as the girls walked down the center of the deserted road. The asphalt had been plowed clear, leaving long drifts of snow along both sides. "I know I just met you and all, but it would be great having someone my age right next door. You have no idea how boring it is living here."

"It's pretty boring living anywhere, isn't it?"

Kathy laughed. "You might have a point."

But a moment later her sunny face darkened. "It didn't used to be so bad, but now that it's just me and Mom, I get lonely all the time."

Melanie sighed. "Yeah," she admitted. "I get lonely too."

But even as nice as her new friend seemed, Melanie didn't expect they'd be able to help each other out with that. The fact was, she *wasn't* moving in next door.

She wasn't even coming back.

"I just can't get over this place," Jesse's mother said scornfully, staring at the Joneses' enormous Tudor mansion through the window of her rented car. "I thought our Malibu house was ostentatious."

"I think Elsa picked it out," Jesse said defensively, wishing he'd insisted on meeting her at her hotel. She'd been bent on coming to get him, though, and he suspected now that her interest in driving had had more to do with seeing her ex's new house than the Missouri countryside.

"I'll bet she did." His mother's tone said more than words.

"I'll see you after school tomorrow," he said quickly. It had already been a long day, and once they got started insulting Elsa, there was no telling how far into the night they could go. "I'll come to the hotel."

He let himself out of the car, hoping to get to his room without running into any of the other residents of his house. He could see a light shining from the den as he crept through the front door into the entryway, but no one appeared. Hurrying up the stairs, Jesse closed his door and leaned against it, breathing a sigh of relief. The last thing he wanted that night was more hassles with his father and Elsa.

Moving away from the door, he fell onto his bed in the darkened room, not bothering to switch on a light. All he wanted was to be alone to think about the day he'd just spent with his mother.

And about moving to California. Because the more he saw of his mom, the more homesick he got for Malibu. They had talked about it a lot that day—the fact that the two of them would have to squeeze into a two-bedroom condominium, whether moving again would decrease his chances of a football scholarship, whether his father would even let him go.

That was the biggest wild card as far as Jesse was concerned. His mother had made it clear that a custody battle was out of the question—she didn't have the money for it, for one thing, and the way things dragged on in court, Jesse could be eighteen before any decision was reached. If his father didn't want to let him go, he could kill the whole plan.

On the other hand, Jesse was sixteen now— practically an adult. If he decided he was leaving, could his father really stop him?

The split-second knock on his door was so unexpected that Jesse didn't even have time to react before Brittany burst in on him.

"Brittany! What do you think you're doing?" he shouted, bounding off the bed. "I told you to stay out of here."

"I knocked."

She looked so fragile standing in his doorway he could almost imagine huffing, and puffing, and blowing her down, just like the Big Bad Wolf.

"I don't care. I don't want you in here. Understand?"

"No," she said stubbornly, her hands on her skinny hips. "I *don't* understand. Why can't I talk to you, Jesse? We used to talk."

"No, we didn't. What dream was that in? Just get out of here now, before I make you."

"You can't make me. I'll call Mom."

Springing forward, he grabbed her slender shoulders and squeezed hard. "You call Elsa, and you'll be sorrier than you can imagine," he promised in a furious whisper. He could feel her bones beneath his hands. He imagined squeezing until something snapped, wondered if he could . . .

"Just get out of here," he said, shoving her roughly out the door and slamming it behind her.

His heart was beating so hard he could feel the blood pulse in his throat. He couldn't believe that for a moment he had actually wanted to hurt her, but his empty hands still clenched at his sides, helpless with rage. He took a few deep breaths, trying to calm himself down.

This isn't me, he thought. *Threatening a ninety-pound girl?*

It wasn't the him he wanted to be anyway. The divorce, moving to Missouri . . . it had all changed him somehow. And the longer he stayed with his father and Elsa, the worse things were likely to get.

Me and Dad are going to end up like Charlie and Coach Davis.

An early divorce, a series of girlfriends and broken promises, and a whole lot of alcohol had killed the last remnants of a relationship between Charlie and his only son. The two kept tabs on each other somehow, but they hadn't spoken since the coach's teenage years. Jesse didn't know all the details, but Charlie had said that Coach Davis considered his stepfather to be his real father now.

And where Charlie was an alcoholic, Dr. Jones was a workaholic—and one with a trophy wife to boot. The close relationship Jesse had once had with his father had probably been mortally wounded by the divorce, but Elsa's daily presence was smothering the last sparks of life from its corpse.

I have to get out of here, Jesse thought desperately. *This place is killing me.*

Eight

"Do I believe my eyes?" Nicole breathed, staring down the main hallway at lunchtime on Monday. "This is too corny for words!"

Courtney and Emily Dooley were walking right toward her, arms linked together, wearing identical NewBoyz concert shirts.

That can't be Courtney.

There was no way her best friend would ever do something so lame. In fact, up until that moment, Nicole had thought even Emily was cooler than that.

It must be some sort of alien replacement thing. Emily's a body snatcher—that has to be it.

"Hi, Nicole!" Courtney sang out as the pair drew nearer. "What are you doing? Holding down the floor?"

Emily giggled as maniacally as if Courtney's comment had actually been funny. "Oh, like that girl at the concert!" she gasped, plucking at Courtney's sleeve. "Remember? She was standing by that thing, and then the thing . . ."

106

"The Milk Duds girl!" they howled together, laughing like idiots.

"Oh! Oh!" Courtney cried. "And what about the other one?"

"The one with the *hair*?" Emily squealed. "Oh, *please*! I could practically cry for her right here."

Nicole's blood boiled as the inside jokes continued with no attempt to fill her in. *If they're looking for an audience*, she thought jealously, *almost anyone else would appreciate their act more than I do.*

But she really couldn't believe that Courtney *did* want an audience, considering the way she was embarrassing herself. Most people had already gone out to lunch, but there were still stragglers left in the hallway to see what fools she and Emily were making of themselves. Nicole remembered a time—and a time not that long ago—when Courtney would have had nothing but scorn for such a phony twin routine.

"It was just a concert," Nicole broke in sulkily. "You guys are carrying on like you met the band."

"You had to be there," Emily said, laying a condescending hand on her arm. "Come to lunch with us, and we'll tell you all about it."

Like I want to hear! Nicole jerked her arm away.

"Yeah, come on, Nicole," Courtney urged. "You won't believe how much fun we had."

"I have some homework to finish before fifth period," Nicole said stiffly. "I'll see you guys around."

They didn't even try to stop her as she stalked off in the direction of the library, but Nicole could hear them laughing at their stupid jokes again.

Or were they laughing at her?

The possibility made her almost too angry to think. *That's it*, she told herself. *That's the final straw.*

And since she'd already made up her mind to stay friends with Courtney, there was only one thing left to do.

I have to get rid of Emily Dooley. Only this time I won't be so nice.

"What are you doing?" a guy's voice asked.

Keeping one hand against the poster he was taping to the wall, Ben turned his head to see who had spoken.

"We're having a Valentine's Day sale," he explained to the stranger standing in the hallway behind him. "To raise money for charity."

"I don't think so! Didn't anybody tell you the ASB was having a Valentine's sale?"

"Yeah, I heard about that. But it doesn't matter."

The guy's brows drew together. "It matters to me. I'm the treasurer of the ASB, and you can't run a sale that competes with ours."

"Just a second." Ben slapped a few more pieces of tape on his computer-generated poster, then turned to face his interrogator again. "We asked Principal Kelly, and he said it was okay."

"Are you kidding me?" the guy demanded. "He said we could have a chocolate sale."

"Exactly. So what's the problem?" Stepping to one side, Ben pointed proudly to the words at the top of his poster:

DON'T <u>BE</u> A SUCKER. BUY ONE!

"You're selling chocolates and we're selling suckers," Ben said, barely able to keep from laughing again as he read his witty slogan. "Completely different things."

"Is that all?" the dark-haired guy asked scornfully. "In that case, I think we can handle the competition."

Without stopping to think, Ben found himself rising to the challenge. "No," he said quickly. "No, we're also selling carnations."

"Whatever. I'm not worried."

"You're not?"

Ben hadn't wanted him to be *worried*, but he didn't want Eight Prime brushed off like losers, either. "Wait until Thursday, then. We're going to sell way more stuff than you guys."

"We'll see," said the treasurer, openly skeptical. He swaggered off down the hall, leaving Ben desperate to think of a comeback.

"We *will* see," Ben shouted at his back. "Our sale is going to blow yours away!"

"Yeah, yeah." The kid raised one dismissive hand without even turning around.

"Hey, everyone," Ben shouted impulsively. School was over, but there were still people in the hall. "Be sure to check out the Eight Prime Valentine's Day sale!"

So many heads turned that Ben's cheeks started to burn, but he pointed determinedly to his poster. "We're going to have the best stuff at the best prices, and it's all for charity."

A few kids snickered, but others nodded as if making a mental note. Encouraged, Ben picked up his backpack and the roll of remaining posters and started down the hall in search of another good place to hang one.

"Don't forget the Eight Prime Valentine's Day sale this Thursday and Friday!" he called out as he walked, growing bolder by the second. "Only a sucker would miss it!"

Jesse parked his car in the Joneses' garage, opened the interior door into the kitchen, and stepped into the middle of a screaming contest.

"This is completely unacceptable, Brittany," Elsa was shouting. "I will *not* have you embarrassing us this way. Sister Eugenie said—"

"I don't care what she said!" Brittany screamed

110

hysterically. "She's a horrible old witch and I hate her!"

"*Brittany!*"

Even Jesse was shocked as he edged past the duo en route to his bedroom. He had no idea what Brittany had done, but screaming at Elsa, not to mention calling one of the nuns a witch, showed far more spine than he'd ever dreamt she had. The irony was that Jesse was convinced she couldn't have done anything nearly so bad at school.

She probably wore the wrong color blouse, he thought, knowing how much Brittany hated the Sacred Heart dress code. *Or hemmed her jumper too short.*

On the other hand, Brittany had definitely cranked the attitude up a notch lately. Maybe she'd actually done something interesting. For a moment, he was tempted to check it out. Then he changed his mind.

Whatever it was, I don't want any part of that drama downstairs. I'm just getting my stuff and leaving, he decided, in a hurry to go meet his mother. *Let Elsa deal with Brittany. It'll give her something useful to do for a change.*

Nine

When Melanie got home from school on Tuesday, the house was quiet as a tomb.

Literally, she couldn't help thinking. *A big concrete monument to Mom.*

She sighed as she climbed the curving marble staircase, knowing her father must be passed out somewhere, back to his old habits. At school, she and Jesse were still ignoring each other, and despite whatever she'd been thinking the trip to Aunt Gwen's might accomplish, once again Melanie was forced to admit that running off to Iowa hadn't solved any of her problems.

Even so, she was glad she had gone. Regardless of Melanie's fears about her mother's side of the family, Aunt Gwen had turned out to be nice. So nice, in fact, that by the time they'd reached the turnoff to Clearwater Crossing on Sunday afternoon, Melanie had found herself wondering why her aunt lived alone.

"How come you never married?" she'd blurted out

in the last ten minutes of the ride, realizing a second too late how rude her question was.

But Gwen had only laughed. "Last time I checked, someone has to ask you first."

Melanie's cheeks had burned at her own insensitivity, and now, looking back, it was the one question she still wished she hadn't asked. How awful to be Gwen's age—how old was she, anyway? Forty?—and never even have been proposed to. It seemed like the adult equivalent of being sixteen and never kissed. Not that there was anything wrong with not being married. From what Melanie had seen so far, a life without men even seemed like a good idea.

Putting her backpack down in her room, she began changing out of the clothes she had worn to school, all the while picturing Aunt Gwen's cottage in Iowa and thinking about something like that for herself someday. Gwen's house wasn't fancy, but it was peaceful. Not just quiet—Melanie took quiet for granted—but settled. At rest in a way she couldn't explain. She closed her eyes and imagined living there, walking down to the little bridge in the afternoons. It would be great having someone like Kathy right next door too. A friend to do things with after school, like go shopping or hang out and gossip about guys . . .

With a start, Melanie realized that she wasn't just thinking about living in a house like Gwen's someday, when she was old. She was thinking about living there now, with Aunt Gwen.

Well, why not? It couldn't be any worse than here. In fact, it could be a lot better.

Nobody knew her in Iowa. Not really. And if everyone was currently a little obsessed with the resemblance between Melanie and her mother, they'd soon lose interest in that.

I could start fresh there. I could blend in. And instead of going out for cheerleader, this time I'd go out of my way to make sure people didn't even know my name.

There would be freedom in that kind of anonymity. To be the watcher instead of the watched . . .

Melanie pulled on a pair of holey blue sweatpants with a pair of thick white socks. There were dozens of cute outfits in her closet, but she was tired of dressing to impress.

Besides, it isn't as if anyone's going to see me, she thought, belly-flopping onto her bed. She'd be surprised if her father roused himself for dinner, and as far as Jesse dropping by . . .

I'm pretty sure he'll never do that again. Even if I want him to.

With a sigh, she rolled over and stared at her white ceiling, seeing the blanket of snow in her aunt Gwen's front yard. When she'd left Iowa on Sunday, Melanie had fully assumed she was never going back.

But now, only two days later, she was already missing the place.

Aunt Gwen did say I was welcome back anytime. She even said she'd drive out and get me again.

And it certainly wasn't as if Melanie had anything else to do. She twisted a ring around her pinkie, still staring into space.

Well . . . maybe just one more trip.

"Get in, get the coat, get out. That's the plan," Jesse reminded himself as he pulled into the garage. "Don't spend one minute longer here than you have to."

He was already annoyed with himself for not having brought his heavy coat to school in the first place; the last thing he needed was an encounter with Elsa or Brittany. At least his father wasn't home, Jesse noted gratefully as he slammed his car door shut. Elsa's black Mercedes was parked in its usual slot, but Dr. Jones's silver one was nowhere in sight. If Jesse hurried, he might be lucky enough to sneak in and out without seeing anyone.

He made it to the stairs undetected, but he still cursed himself for his own stupidity as he ran up to his room. He knew the weather in Clearwater Crossing changed by the minute—hadn't he given his mother that very lecture? So that morning, when it had seemed so clear and sunny outside, he should have realized he'd be freezing his butt off by noon. Instead he had worn just his letterman's jacket, even though he could easily have put an extra coat in the trunk of his car.

Knowing Mom, she's sure to want to go hiking, or sightseeing, or something that involves getting as cold as possible, he thought as he reached his room. He'd seen more of Clearwater Crossing since she'd been in town than in the whole year he'd lived there without her. She seemed to be packing in every imaginable sight, and even a few Jesse wouldn't have imagined, like the Laura Ingalls Wilder museum over in Mansfield and a tour of the water tower downtown. She was really getting a kick out of country life. *I'm sure it's all very quaint when you don't actually live here.*

Jesse's room was a disaster, but he didn't stop to pick it up. Throwing his backpack into the center of his unmade bed, he kicked off his wet shoes and socks and put on some dry ones. Then he grabbed his heavy coat off the chair and headed back downstairs. To his relief, there was still no sign of the female members of his household as he hustled through the entry on his way to the garage. Just a few more feet and he'd be . . .

"What the—?"

Jesse froze in the doorway between the house and garage, completely stunned. He had parked his immaculately clean BMW in its regular space not five minutes before. But now . . .

There was only one person who could be responsible for such a crime.

"*Brittany!*" he hollered at the top of his lungs. "Brittany, get your scrawny butt down here *now!*"

Elsa appeared instead. "What's the matter?"

"What's the *matter?*" Jesse shouted, still unable to believe his eyes. "Your little brat shaving-creamed my car!"

His finger shook with rage as he pointed at the mess his stepsister had made. "What is *wrong* with that kid?"

"Don't use that tone of voice with me," Elsa warned, bristling.

"I'll use whatever tone I want!" he yelled right in her face. "What are you going to do about it?"

Elsa stepped backward. "I'll tell your father."

"Oh, way to go, Elsa. Way to handle it," he sneered, his voice oozing the hatred he felt.

"I'm *going* to handle it, and I don't need any lip from you," she said, wheeling around to call back into the house. "Brittany! Brittany, you come here right now!"

Jesse's hands clenched into fists as he stared at the streaks of white foam marring his red paint and the wild waves and loops across his windows. How had she made such a big mess in so little time?

She must have been hiding out, just waiting for me to come home, he realized.

But what he couldn't understand was what had provoked such an unwarranted attack. Maybe he and Brittany had been arguing a little more than usual lately, but that was still no excuse for *this*.

This means war, he thought, touching a finger to the goo on his hood. *I swear I'm going to*—

"What?" Brittany said from behind him.

"What?" he repeated in a rage, whirling around to confront her. "What about this? That's what!"

Brittany stood to one side of the doorway, only her head and shoulders showing through the opening. She looked so small and terrified that for a moment, Jesse almost pitied her.

Then he looked at his car again.

"I don't know what's going on in your tiny excuse for a brain," he shouted, "but if that stuff dulls the paint, you're dead!"

"I—I didn't do it," she whimpered.

"Do you see anyone else around here? Besides, there's shaving cream on your dress, you idiot."

Brittany froze, then slowly looked down at the telltale spot of foam on her school jumper, bursting into tears at the sight. Jesse hesitated, still full of things he wanted to shout at her. The adrenaline rushing through his body made him nearly desperate to do something.

"Brittany, I don't know what's gotten into you

118

lately," Elsa scolded. "This isn't how I raised you. You ought to be ashamed of yourself!"

Jesse supposed she meant her tone to convey the seriousness of the situation, but to his ears it was just witchy and condescending and nearly impossible to listen to. Brittany needed a good chewing out, not Elsa's version of child psychology. Yanking the driver's side door open, he jumped in and screeched the BMW backward onto the driveway.

Elsa was yelling and Brittany was wailing as he got out and dragged the hose over to spray down his car. Jesse tried to ignore the commotion in the garage while his fingers slowly froze in the dripping stream and water soaked the leather of his second pair of shoes.

There's not a city in the world that's far enough away from here, but Malibu's about as good as it gets, he thought, feeling an almost unbearable urge to be already there.

Brittany screamed her excuses in the garage. Elsa hollered back. A door slammed.

Jesse closed his eyes, drawing a deep breath as the diluted shaving cream gathered in a pool around his cold, wet feet.

These people were practically making his decision for him.

"Do you think we should call Nicole before we do this?" Peter asked, hesitating with a can of red spray paint in his hand. "I mean, do you think she'll mind?"

"Why would she?" Jenna replied. "She gave this table to Eight Prime. Besides, we already bought the paint."

The two of them were standing in the Altmanns' garage that Tuesday evening, looking down on a square island of a card table lost in a newspaper sea. To keep the garage clean, the duo had spread old papers all over the concrete floor and taped them halfway up the walls in the corner they were using. The cars had been moved outside.

Peter grinned. "That's right. It would be a shame to waste our three fifty," he teased. "Much better to lose a friend."

"Over this?" Jenna shook her head. "No way. Just do it."

"If she gets mad, remember this was your idea," Peter said, pressing down on the spray button. A bright swath of red settled out across the surface of the beat-up old table, hiding a variety of multi-colored scuffs and stains.

"I'll be *happy* to take the credit, because it's looking better already."

"That's not saying much," Peter remarked, continuing to spray in long, even swipes.

Jenna stood watching with satisfaction as the paint went down in a glistening layer. Making the table red for the Valentine's Day sale had been her idea, and she was still sure it was a good one. She could already envision how great their booth would look when they put a few buckets of red, pink, and white carnations out in front of the table, with white paper doilies and the red heart-shaped suckers on top.

"Let's paint the cash box too," she said impulsively. "I'm telling you, Nicole won't care!" she added as Peter raised an eyebrow at her. "And that way everything will match."

"I suppose it could use a coat of something to glue that rust together," Peter said grudgingly. "You take over here, and I'll go get it."

He handed her the spray can and pointed. "Why don't you start on the legs and let the top dry for a while? We want to paint lightly so we don't end up with runs."

Jenna hummed as the leg she was painting turned from rusty gray to glossy red. By the time Peter returned, she was working on a second one.

"Hey, that's starting to look pretty good!" he said.

"I told you," she said happily.

Jenna continued to paint while Peter laid out more newspaper, then began rubbing a lump of steel wool over the outside of Eight Prime's old cash box.

"Hoping for a genie?" she teased.

"Nope," Peter replied with a smile. "I have everything I need right here."

She could feel herself blushing, but instead of

hiding her face, she smiled back. "So where are we going for Valentine's Day? Come on, I'm dying to know."

"You don't really want me to tell you. It would ruin the surprise."

"No, I do. I *really* do."

Peter laughed. "Too bad. You'll have to wait and see."

Jenna racked her brain for a way to persuade him. "But if I don't know where I'm going, how will I know what to wear?"

"I'm pretty sure you already picked something out."

Too late, she remembered she'd told him about her shopping trip with Caitlin.

"Ohhh!" she groaned. "Then at least tell me if we're going to the same place as Caitlin and David."

"You ask too many questions. I'd rather surprise you."

"You know I hate surprises," she whined. "The suspense is going to kill me."

Peter rolled his eyes. "You love surprises. You just hate not knowing what they are." Opening the cash box wide, he flipped it upside down on the paper he'd spread out. "Okay, you might as well hit this next."

Jenna put a few last touches on the fourth table leg and moved to spray the old box, her mind still full of her impending date with Peter. There was nothing she wouldn't give to find out what they'd be doing

122

Sunday night, but at the same time she had to admit that it *was* kind of exciting not knowing. She set herself to imagining the most perfect, most private, most romantic . . .

"Boy, that old cash box has seen a few things," Peter said nostalgically, jolting Jenna back to the reality of moving the paint over its surface. "I remember when Nicole brought it to our very first event—the car wash, remember?"

"How could I forget?"

Of all the fund-raisers Eight Prime had held, the car wash had been Jenna's least favorite. Of course, at the time she'd been hopelessly brokenhearted about Miguel's new relationship with Leah, which might have had something to do with her attitude.

"We sure have accomplished a lot since then," Peter said, a faraway smile on his face. "Every time I see that bus . . ."

He didn't finish the sentence, but Jenna knew what he meant. Everything about Eight Prime seemed miraculous to both of them. That eight such different people would meet at all, let alone agree to work together, was strange enough. But the fact that everything they'd done had been so successful made her and Peter both believe there was another, unseen member of the group—one who was supporting them every step of the way.

"I wish I wasn't so worried about Ben ordering the stuff for the sale," Peter said, striking a sour note. "I

123

keep telling myself that everything always goes fine. But then again, it's *Ben*. And, well . . . maybe we shouldn't have let him handle things on his own."

Jenna put the final spurt of red on the cash box and rose from her knees to face Peter. "It's a little late to start worrying now. He told me he already sent in the order."

"I know," Peter said with a grimace. "And I feel lousy questioning him. It's just that, well . . ."

"I know."

Ben was the least mature, clumsiest, most disaster-prone member of the group. At every fund-raiser Eight Prime had ever been involved with, he'd spilled or stained or splatted or—

"I'd hate to have him think we don't *trust* him," Peter said. "But maybe we ought to give him a call and just ask him if he needs any help."

"Help with what?"

Peter shook his head. "I don't know. How about getting the candy and flowers to school on Thursday morning? He's going to have at least three of those big white buckets, don't you think? Plus the suckers? How's he going to handle all that?"

Jenna considered the situation. She definitely understood Peter's concern, but Ben had assured them all repeatedly that he had everything under control. There was no way she and Peter could break into things now without hurting his feelings.

Besides, what could really go wrong? she thought. *He buys a few things, he brings them to school. We'll all be there to help with the rest.*

She shook her head. "You worry too much," she told Peter. "Give Ben a chance to be the hero for a change."

Ten

"**I**s Neil picking you up tonight?" Nicole asked Gail as they walked toward the street after their Wednesday shift. Darkness had fallen, and so had the temperature, tempting Nicole to bum a ride home if she could.

Gail shook her head and headed for the bus stop down the block. "I don't want Neil coming around here for a while. Not with . . ." She hesitated, then jerked her head back toward Wienerageous. "You know."

Not really, thought Nicole, walking along at her cousin's heels. When the whole affair with Mr. Roarke had begun, Nicole had thought she understood the rules, but now they seemed to be changing daily.

"I, uh—I thought Neil didn't know you were dating Mr. Roarke," she said, completely confused.

Gail grimaced. "He doesn't. But it turns out Mr. Roarke knows about me and Neil. I swear the creep has no life at all."

"But . . . how did he find out?"

"Spying. The usual. He's seen Neil pick me up and he put two and two together."

The girls reached the bus stop. Instead of standing at the curb, though, they huddled in the shelter of the adjacent drugstore, their coats wrapped tightly around them. They were awaiting buses headed in different directions, but Nicole knew they'd see them coming in plenty of time for her to cross the street to catch hers.

"So, you're telling me he knew you had a boyfriend and he wanted to date you anyway?" she said. "What is this guy's problem?"

Gail laughed without smiling. "Take your pick. I really wish he didn't know about Neil, though. It only makes things harder."

"You don't think he'll tell Neil?"

"No. He just says scuzzy things about us."

"Like what?"

"Like 'Don't act so innocent with me. I've seen that guy you hang out with.' He turns my stomach."

"Mine too."

"The most ridiculous part is that he claims he knows what I'm *really* like." Gail shook her head. "As if that's possible. *I* don't even know what I'm like anymore. Everything's just gotten so . . . I don't know. Pointless."

Nicole shivered, and more from her cousin's tired, defeated tone than the cold. "Pointless?" she repeated.

"It's just so hard to take anything seriously, you know? I mean, nobody cares. All they care about are a few arbitrary rules, and maybe making some money and not looking too pathetic in front of their friends. That's it."

"That's not true!" Nicole protested. "People care." But the jaded expression in her cousin's blue eyes made her feel like Pollyanna.

"Right. Sure they do," Gail said with a sardonic smile. "But don't worry, Nicole—it's not like I can't take care of myself. I know how things work in this world."

If you do, then you're one up on me.

But Nicole didn't want to admit how young and scared she suddenly felt. What had once seemed like the only way out of a bad situation—having Gail date Mr. Roarke—now seemed worse than the trouble they'd tried to avoid. Gail had changed in the last few days. Not only didn't her super-sweet act shine the way it once had, the mischievous side of her personality had been completely crushed. It was almost as if she were punishing herself—although that didn't make sense, either, with Mr. Roarke already so firmly on the job.

"I don't think you should go out with Mr. Roarke anymore," Nicole said impulsively.

"Neither do I. But we have another date tomorrow."

"Don't go, Gail. He's just so . . . I don't know. I hate to say it, but maybe we should tell our parents after all. Or, I know! *Tell* him you're going to tell. Call his bluff."

Nicole grabbed at her cousin's sleeve, excited by her own idea. "That's it! Tell him you dated him and you're done. If he tells on you now, you'll tell on him."

For a moment, a flicker of life entered her cousin's eyes. Then she shook her head.

"It's more complicated than that," she said, reverting to her former depression. "He can fire me anytime just by saying my work has slipped. And he can tell my parents about Neil, and a lot more than that I gave away a few free burgers. And even if I told on him, who would believe me? He's the boss and I'm just a kid." She shook her head again. "No, I have to stay on his good side."

A rumble down the street announced the approach of Gail's bus.

"Are you sure?" Nicole asked as it rolled to the stop. "Think about it, Gail."

"I have to go. I'll see you at work on Friday." Shrugging Nicole's hand from her sleeve, Gail climbed aboard.

"I just don't think you should go out with that barracuda when you're already feeling so down," Nicole called after her, earning a strange look from the driver.

I don't think you should go out with anyone, she added silently as the bus drove away. Pulling her coat closer, she huddled down into its warmth and crossed the street.

I don't think we made the right decision.

Everything was spiraling out of control, and Nicole was afraid for her cousin. If Gail had even just admitted that things were out of hand, Nicole would have felt better. At least they'd have been in agreement. But how could Gail keep insisting she was handling things when nothing was being handled?

Nicole shivered again. *I really hope she knows what she's doing.*

"I'll get it!" Ben hollered, thundering down the stairs from his room to the Pipkins' front door. "It's for me!"

Barreling around the corner, he screeched up to the door, barely managing to stop before he ran into the wood. The man on the outdoor side was wearing the familiar brown uniform of the local delivery service, and beside him on the doorstep were two long cardboard boxes.

"Is your dad here?" he asked, glancing down at his digital pad. "I have a delivery for Ben Pipkin."

"That's me. I mean, it's my dad's name, too, but he's the senior and I'm the junior, and . . ."

Why was he going into all this? "Those are for me," Ben finished, pointing to the boxes. "I'm the one who ordered them."

The delivery man looked skeptical, but he held his pad out to Ben. "Then you need to sign right here while I get more boxes out of the truck."

Ben signed eagerly, pulling the first two boxes inside while the driver went after the others. The man came back with another long box as well as two much smaller square ones.

"Okay, here you go. Five total." Putting the rest of the packages down, he took his pad back from Ben and checked to make sure it was signed in the right place. "Have a nice day."

"Yeah, you too," Ben echoed distractedly, bringing in the last boxes, then shutting the door.

The big boxes must be the flowers, he thought, lifting one of the small ones, *and these must be the suckers*.

A quick rattle confirmed his theory, and Ben carried the box into the kitchen, where he could use a knife to cut the tape. The flowers were going to require trimming and watering, but the suckers would be ready to sell, and he couldn't wait to see them.

"This is going to be so cool!" he said, getting the box top open and snatching out a handful of packing paper. "I can't wait until . . . *What?* Oh, no!"

The room spun sickeningly as he stared down at the first two hundred and fifty suckers. "No, this can't be happening."

They were green.

They can't *be green*, he thought, fighting for air. *How can they be green?*

Still holding the knife, Ben hurried back to the entry and stabbed into the other small box, scattering tape, cardboard, and packing paper everywhere in his frenzy.

Also green.

"This is so wrong," he moaned, yanking the front door open. Maybe he could still stop the delivery man and find out what to do. . . .

But the big brown truck was gone.

Okay. Stay calm, he told himself, ignoring the fact that he was already anything but. *This is just a minor snag. You'll think of a way to fix it.*

In the meantime, he needed to get the flowers into water. Sitting on the floor, he cut the tape on the first big box, peeling back wet plastic to reveal the carnations underneath.

Lavender. All three bundles.

"No, this isn't happening!" he cried. "Why do these things always happen to *me*?"

The flowers in the other two boxes were lavender as well—eight bundles, all the exact same color.

Eight Prime is going to kill *me!* he thought. *Or kick me out at the very least. No one will ever believe this wasn't my fault.*

Hacking the plastic envelope containing the packing slip off one of the large boxes, Ben studied it for some clue as to what had happened. The document wasn't specific enough to help him, though, showing only an order for five hundred suckers and two hundred carnations without mentioning their colors. Clutching the slip of paper, Ben charged up the stairs to his room and flipped on his computer. Could he have misentered some important number? But how could he have messed up the candy *and* the flowers? A chimp could enter data better than that.

Logging on to the Internet, Ben found the site he had ordered from and scanned through the screens until he found the red heart-shaped suckers and the red, pink, white, and peppermint carnations he had intended to order.

"I did it right!" he exclaimed with relief, double-checking his packing slip. "They're the ones who messed up!"

He had given the right item numbers; someone had packed the boxes wrong. He should have realized before that lavender carnations couldn't have four different item numbers, but he'd been so freaked out by the sight of them he hadn't even noticed.

"It's their mistake," he said happily. "They'll have to make it right."

Scrolling through the order form he had filled out before, Ben kept his eyes open for a toll-free number he could use to call the company. With the Eight Prime sale supposed to begin the next day, he needed to talk to customer service, and he needed to talk to them *now*.

"There's got to be a phone number here somewhere," he muttered. But he scrolled all the way through the order form without finding one, ending up in the screens of explanatory data he had skipped before. "Maybe somewhere in these stupid instructions . . ."

Ben scanned down the lines of ordering information, still amazed by the unnecessary amount of detail. And then he noticed something: the farther down the screens he got, the more the words *No Refunds* started to jump out at him. They seemed to be at the end of every line, notching up his adrenaline by degrees.

But that's all right, because it's their mistake, he reassured himself, wiping the sweat from his forehead. *They sent the wrong thing, so they can't expect me to—*

His brain froze in midthought as his eyes hit the final paragraph:

DUE TO THE HIGH SEASONAL DEMAND FOR CERTAIN ITEMS, WE RESERVE THE RIGHT TO SUBSTITUTE COLORS AS NECESSARY. THE PURCHASER'S SIGNATURE OF ACCEPTANCE OF THE PACKAGE IS ALSO DEEMED ACCEPTANCE OF ANY COLOR SUBSTITUTIONS. ITEMS ARE PERISHABLE, SO DO NOT SIGN FOR PACKAGES UNTIL YOU HAVE INSPECTED THEIR CONTENTS. *NO REFUNDS!*

Ben's head dropped into his hands. He'd spent the group's money, he couldn't get it back, and now Eight Prime was holding a Valentine's Day sale with green suckers and purple flowers. Not only that, but he'd put up posters all over school and bragged to everyone who would listen about how Eight Prime's sale would beat the ASB's.

Maybe it will still be okay, he thought desperately taking a deep breath. *Maybe people will like the . . .*

Oh, who am I kidding? I'm dead.

"How kind of you to grace us with your presence, Jesse," Elsa said snidely from across the table. "Did your mother have other plans tonight?"

Jesse shot her an evil look. "Not at all. Do you want me to call and invite her over?"

Brittany looked silently from one to the other, as if fearing a repeat of the shouting match of the day before. Elsa had bawled her out good for the shaving-cream incident, but Jesse still wasn't satisfied. It had been clear to him that Elsa's anger had had much more to do with Brittany making her look bad than with any actual concern for damage to his car. Whatever her motives had been, however, she seemed to have made her point—no one had heard a peep out of Brittany for nearly twenty-four hours.

"Shut your mouth and pass the potatoes," Dr. Jones growled at him, reaching for the dish.

135

Jesse grudgingly handed them over.

"So when is Beth going home, anyway?" his father asked, piling potatoes onto his plate. "It seems like she's been here forever."

"She's leaving on Monday, same as every time you ask me," Jesse said through clenched teeth.

"I guess you can keep any schedule you like when you don't have a job," Elsa said.

"You should talk!" Jesse said, too angry to be cautious. "At least my mom helped *earn* the money she's living on. Besides, Monday is a holiday."

Elsa looked ready to slap him. Her icy blue eyes narrowed as she drew up to full height in her chair.

"You apologize to your mother!" Dr. Jones barked.

"My mother isn't here."

"Don't split hairs with me," Dr. Jones said furiously. "I swear I'll—"

But Jesse didn't wait for the rest of the threat. "All right, then, Elsa. I'm sorry. I'm sorry I ever met you, all right? But I'm going to do us all a big favor: When my mom leaves town on Monday, I'm going with her. I'm moving back to Malibu."

"Like hell you are!" his father exploded. "That's not your decision to make, and it's not your mother's either. There are laws, you know."

But Jesse was so fed up that the question of formal custody seemed more like an annoyance than any real impediment. "How are you going to stop me if I decide I'm leaving?" he shouted. "You're not even around enough to notice I'm missing."

"Well, I can start by taking away your car," Dr. Jones shot back with the veins standing out in his neck.

"Do it, and I'm gone the same day," Jesse promised. "I don't need a car to get out of here."

They faced off, each waiting for the other to back down or show any sign of weakness, when an unexpected commotion erupted at the table. Brittany burst into tears.

Her sobs were loud and sudden, as if she'd held them back until the last possible second. Jumping up, she scraped her chair loudly against the wooden floor. Her face was red, her eyes streaming as she took one last look around the table then ran out of the room, leaving her untouched plate behind.

"Oh, for crying out loud. What's the little prima donna's problem now?" Dr. Jones demanded. "I swear, Elsa, that kid of yours . . ."

His wife gave him the type of look she'd directed at Jesse earlier, then got up to follow her daughter.

Jesse suddenly realized he was sitting alone with his father—the last person he wanted to talk to. Rising abruptly, he stalked out of the dining room in the other direction, toward the garage.

Sinking into the cool leather sanctuary of his BMW, Jesse slammed the driver's door and started the engine. He turned up the radio to drown out the noise in his head, then punched the garage door opener. The metal door rolled up and he backed into the driveway without the least clue where he was going.

It was early enough that he could still go visit his mother at her hotel. He'd have gone there in the first place if his father and Elsa hadn't been giving him so much flak about missing dinners. But he didn't want to head straight there—not the way he was feeling.

I'll drive around for a while, he thought. *No one is expecting me, so I can do whatever I want.*

He rolled slowly down his darkened street to the corner, where instead of turning right, toward the lake, he found himself turning left.

Toward Melanie's house.

If you're even thinking about stopping there, you're a fool, he told himself, continuing to drive in that direction. *How many times does she have to dump on you before you take the hint?*

On the other hand, he didn't actually have to stop. Melanie's bedroom was at the front of the house. He could just drive by and see if her light was on.

Not that that would accomplish anything.

Not that he could resist the temptation.

You are one pathetic chump, he thought, still driving. *You never acted like this about the girls you knew in California.*

And he'd known a lot of them, too. What did Melanie Andrews have that he hadn't seen a hundred times before?

He pulled a sudden U-turn in the center of the deserted road, heading back toward his mother's hotel.

Nothing, that's what. And if there were more cute girls in this Podunk town, I'd have forgotten her already. The sooner I get out of Clearwater Crossing, the better!

Eleven

Nicole didn't hesitate when she saw Courtney and Emily on the lawn in front of the high school Thursday morning. Tossing her head determinedly, she moved to intercept them before they could reach the main building.

"Hi!" she called, trotting the last few feet. Forcing a friendly smile to her lips, she made sure her voice oozed honey. "Nice day, huh?"

Courtney blinked, and apparently more from surprise than the February sunshine. "Pretty nice, I guess."

"So what are we doing this afternoon?" Nicole asked, shifting her gaze from Courtney to Emily.

Her rival was wearing red that day, a far cry from the unrelenting pastels of junior high. Her short brown hair was moussed and studded with butterfly pins, a style Nicole herself had tried unsuccessfully to copy from that month's *Modern Girl* magazine.

"Hi, Nicole!" she said, all sugar. "Don't you look nice today."

Nicole put a self-conscious hand to her windblown hair, then jerked it back down again. Emily wasn't going to rattle her that easily. "Thanks."

"I thought you were selling suckers with the God Squad today," Courtney said.

"That's right, I am!" Nicole said brightly, all ready with her answer. "And I hope you're both going to buy some. You know what a good cause it is."

"Maybe, if we have time during lunch," Emily said. "We're going shopping right after school."

"Oh, good. I'll go with you." Spending a precious rare afternoon off with Emily Dooley was hardly Nicole's idea of fun, but somehow she managed to keep the smile on her face and think of the larger plan. Sooner or later, Emily would let down her guard, and then—

"You just said you were selling suckers," Courtney protested. "How are you going to go shopping?"

"The after-school part of the sale only lasts until people clear out of the building. If you two can't wait fifteen minutes for charity . . . ," Nicole said, hoping to make them feel guilty.

"For charity?" Courtney said skeptically. "I thought we were waiting fifteen minutes for you."

"Judging by that outfit, it would be the same thing," Emily said, giggling. "No offense, Nicole. I couldn't resist."

"Yeah. Very funny." Nicole tried to act like she could take a joke, but inside she was burning up. If Emily had had to help Ajax change the oil in the

141

deep fryers the night before, then spent another hour getting the smell out from under her nails, she wouldn't have had time to coordinate her accessories either.

"All right," Courtney relented. "If you're sure you want to come with us, we'll wait for you in the parking lot."

"Why *wouldn't* I want to come?" Nicole turned a big, fake smile on Emily, inviting her to answer. If she would only say she didn't want Nicole along, then Courtney would have to see who was really to blame for their feud. . . .

But Emily didn't rise to the bait. "That's right!" she said with an equally fake smile. "There's no reason the three of us can't do things together. After all, this isn't junior high. We're all a lot more mature now."

"Exactly," said Nicole. "No one owns anyone else."

Courtney looked from one to the other, a cynical smile on her lips. "Sure. We're all just one big, happy family."

Yanking a heavy door open, she let the three of them into the heated hall. "This ought to be interesting."

"It's really not that bad," Jenna whispered to Ben, her heart nearly breaking for him. The poor guy was already a wreck about the mistake with the flowers and suckers, and the only "business" at Eight Prime's sale so far had been the students stopping by to make fun of the disastrous color choices. Worse, Jenna couldn't help noticing that plenty of the kids walking past without pausing were carrying the small heart-shaped boxes of chocolates being sold by the ASB.

"Are you kidding me?" Ben moaned. "It's a disaster. You're just being nice."

"Well . . . maybe a little nice," Jenna admitted. "But our sale *is* for charity, so maybe people will cut us some slack. You never know."

"*I* know," Jesse said loudly. "I can't believe you did this to us, Ben."

"It's *embarrassing*," added Nicole, one hand shading her eyes.

Leah, Melanie, and Miguel stared off into space, making an obvious effort to keep their mouths shut. Everyone had already given Ben their opinions of his shopping skills—to say anything more at this point was simply rubbing it in.

"Look, we can't fix it," Peter reasoned, "so we'll have to make the best of it."

"No kidding," Jesse said sarcastically.

Not wanting to hear any more, Jenna stepped around to the front of their newly red table and busied herself rearranging the flowers in the three white buckets, trying to make them as attractive as possible. "Well, one good thing is, the carnations are really fresh."

"They're *purple*!" said Nicole.

"I hope they're fresh enough to last until Easter," Miguel said glumly. "Maybe then we'll have a chance."

"I'm sorry!" Ben apologized again. "But I really did do everything right. How was I supposed to know that they'd swap all those colors on me?"

Nobody answered as Jenna surveyed her work, hoping for a miracle. Eight Prime had set up shop in an alcove beside the cafeteria's main entrance. Normally it would have been a perfect location, directly in sight of everyone who walked in. Unfortunately, this was the one time the group would have loved to be invisible. Looking at their booth now, Jenna could barely remember the red, white, and pink fantasy she'd envisioned when she and Peter had painted the card table. The lavender flowers clashed fiercely with the red paint, and the green suckers on top looked more like petrified hunks of cough syrup than something a person might actually eat.

Of all the colors candy comes in, she thought, shaking her head. *Does* anybody *like green?*

Her attention was diverted by Melanie calling out to a group of football players.

"Hey, you guys! How about some flowers for your

Valentines?" she suggested, putting on a flirtatious smile. "We have suckers, too."

The guys glanced at the table, then laughed. "No thanks," one of them answered, turning his attention to Jesse instead. "Purple and green for Valentine's Day? You need to study your holidays, Jones."

"It's for charity," Melanie reminded them quickly, but they just waved her off and walked into the cafeteria.

"We're doomed!" Ben wailed. "If Melanie can't sell this stuff, none of us can."

"Thanks for the vote of confidence," Nicole grumbled.

Jesse shot Ben a lethal look.

"We just need a better plan." Leah pointed over her shoulder at the signs taped to the wall behind her. "Something a little more aggressive than posters."

"We could cut our prices," Miguel suggested.

"Let's save that idea for later," Peter said. "We haven't even been here ten minutes yet."

"And we haven't sold a single thing," Jesse countered, as if they needed the reminder. "In a couple more minutes, everyone is going to be eating and we'll be standing here for no reason."

"We should split up," Jenna suggested. "Why don't you guys take some of these suckers around to the tables and see if you have better luck selling them as dessert?"

"Why don't you girls?" Jesse retorted.

"Fine," Nicole told him. "You can carry some flowers, then."

"I'm not walking around with any flowers!"

"All right. Let's not panic," said Peter. "We don't want the flowers out of water anyway."

"*I'll* take the suckers," Jenna said. "Do you want to help me, Peter?"

"Sure."

They each grabbed double handfuls of the spherical green suckers, even though Jenna was starting to believe they'd be lucky to sell ten. Still, anything was better than hanging around the booth, listening to Eight Prime tear itself down. She and Peter walked to the edge of the tables and stood looking at the crowd.

"What do you think we should do?" she asked. "Pace back and forth and hope somebody stops us, like the peanut guy at a ball game?"

"I don't think we'll get that lucky. We'll have to make up a slogan or something to call out as we go."

They both grimaced at the idea of drawing that much attention to themselves—especially when all they had to offer were putrid green suckers.

"Peter, what if we don't sell this stuff?" Jenna blurted out, voicing the fear that had dogged her since the moment she'd first seen Ben's purchases. "We've always been lucky before, but this time . . . I really don't know."

"It doesn't look good," he admitted. "If things don't pick up soon, we could lose all our money."

Jenna hated to think how her friends would react to that. Eight Prime had seen its ups and downs, but the group had never actually failed. Not only that, but everyone had used their own money this time—and there was nothing in the bank account to pay themselves back with. The cash they'd be losing from Christmas and birthdays was a big chunk of what most of them had saved.

"Suckers!" she called out suddenly. "Get your Valentine's suckers right here!"

Maybe it was inevitable that Eight Prime would fail sooner or later. And maybe this was the time. But Jenna wasn't going down without a fight.

Jesse pulled into his driveway a little earlier than he had on previous evenings, intending to go straight to bed. Still in a bad mood about the Eight Prime sale earlier that day, he'd declined his mom's offer of dinner at a fancy restaurant, taking her instead for pizza at Slice of Rome. The crowd had been light that Thursday, and the food had been served almost immediately.

"Do you want to see a movie later?" his mother had asked over salad. "I noticed a theater down the block."

But Jesse had shaken his head. "Not tonight. I had a lousy day, and I'm not looking forward to tomorrow, either. I just want to go to bed."

"Is something wrong?" she'd asked with a worried frown.

"Just the usual. School stinks." He didn't feel like going into details about the Valentine's Day sale, and he certainly didn't want to tell her about all the strife her being in town had caused at home.

"Well, do you want to get together tomorrow?" she asked, looking mildly offended. "Or would you rather have a night off?"

"It's not you, Mom," he'd said. The last thing he needed was for her to turn sensitive on him on top of everything else. "I'm just tired. That's all."

Now, sitting in his driveway, he knew how true his words had been. The stress of the last few days had worn him out, and tomorrow he and Eight Prime had to sell those stupid suckers and flowers again, despite the fact that they'd sold almost none so far.

The BMW's headlights hit the back wall of the garage as the door rolled up, flooding it with light. Jesse flipped them off, only to find that the overhead bulb on the door opener had burned out, leaving the garage in near total darkness. The open door behind him let in barely enough light to make out the black silhouettes of things inside. He shuffled cautiously over the concrete, not wanting to bark his shins. As he neared the door into the house, though, a noise behind him made him freeze.

There was something in the garage.

Don't panic, he told himself, heart racing. *It's probably just an animal. Maybe a possum, or a raccoon. They have raccoons in Missouri, right?*

He didn't know, but even a hungry wolf beat the other possibility—a human prowler. Turning very, very slowly, Jesse peered fearfully toward the darkest, most distant corner of the big three-car garage.

"I know you're there," he said, his voice full of false bravado.

The thing in the corner moved again, very slowly, very stealthily. No animal moved like that. Jesse's pulse thudded in his ears as he backed slowly toward the door, trying to think of something to grab for a weapon.

Or should he make a break for the house, bolt the door behind him, and call 911? Their cars were in the garage, so he knew his father and Elsa were home. The three of them could probably handle any burglar crazy enough to try to crash through a locked door.

Keeping his eyes on the corner, Jesse reached behind him and found the doorknob. The door to the house opened, letting light from inside pour into the garage. The added illumination was just enough for him to make out a shape crouched low on the other side of his father's Mercedes, both arms over its blond head.

"Brittany, you moron!" he shouted, finding a switch for another light inside the garage and slamming the door to the house shut again. "What are you doing out here? I could have shot you or something."

Brittany huddled in place a moment, then rose unsteadily to her feet. "You don't have a gun," she said, blinking in the sudden light.

"Lucky for you," he said, still shaky from the adrenaline rushing through his veins. "You want to tell me why you're out here?"

"No." With a remarkably scornful look, she began moving toward the doorway.

For two or three steps she managed a perfect imitation of her mother's haughty walk. Then her feet seemed to fall out of sync with her knees, flopping loose on rubbery legs. She lurched off balance, her scrawny shoulder catching him in the chest as she tried to claw her way back up his body.

"Get off of me!" he said with a push.

For a moment she stood on her own again, full of false dignity. Then she staggered backward.

"Oops!" She giggled, fighting for balance. A second later she collided with the tool bench, laughing hysterically as she clung to it for support.

"You're drunk!" Jesse gasped. He never would have believed it, but here he was, staring at the evidence with his own eyes. And if anyone knew the signs, it was him.

Rushing to the corner where he'd first spotted Brittany, he glimpsed the heel of a dark green bottle protruding from beneath a trash bag. He reached down and grabbed it, pulling it into the light. A couple of inches of wine sloshed in the bottom.

"Are you crazy?" he demanded, holding it out to her. "What are you doing? Sitting here drinking in the dark?"

Her hips braced on the bench, Brittany had finally achieved an upright position. "You do it," she accused.

"I do not!"

"Maybe not in the garage." Reaching forward, she tried to pull the bottle from his hand. "Give me that."

"No way. I'm taking this upstairs to show Dad and Elsa."

She stared him down a moment; then all her false courage left her.

"You big hypocrite!" she said, starting to cry. "You drink all the time."

"For crying out loud, Bee, you're only twelve!" he said, too bothered by her behavior to waste time explaining how wrong she was. "What's the *matter* with you lately? You're acting like a psycho."

The question only made her cry harder. Ignoring him completely, she clung to the edge of the bench, sobbing as if she barely even remembered he was there.

"Okay. Okay, listen," he said awkwardly, moving to stand in front of her. He hesitated, then set the wine down on the bench at her side. "I'm not going to tell anyone. But only if you promise that you'll never do this again."

"I'm not promising you anything."

"Fine." He reached for the bottle, prepared to take it upstairs, but before he could touch it, she threw herself into his arms.

"All right! Just don't tell on me, Jesse. Don't tell Mom and Dad."

He squirmed uncomfortably, not liking so much contact. How could he rat her out when she was clinging to him that way? Not to mention that he was the worst possible person to raise the subject of drinking with their parents. They'd be so angry that, given his past history, the entire incident was certain to backlash on him.

"I won't tell *this* time," he said at last. "But you have to shape up."

He thought he'd given her what she wanted, but instead of letting go, she increased her grip, still sobbing. He looked down at the head bobbing on his shoulder, the freckled nose running onto his shirt, and slowly, uncertainly, patted her back a few times, trying to calm her down. It was an unbearably awkward moment, with a girl he suddenly realized he barely knew at all. Reluctantly, he circled his arms around her, offering what comfort he could.

I don't want this, he thought, wishing he'd gone to the movies with his mother after all. *I don't want to know what's going on in her head. I don't want to know her.*

He had enough problems of his own without getting tangled up in Brittany's. He counted the seconds until he could release her and resume his separate life, her bottle of wine in his sight the whole time.

I wonder how she got that. No, wait. I don't want to know.

He didn't want to know what Brittany did, how she did it, where she did it, or anything about her. He certainly didn't want anyone blaming her bad decisions on him.

Like she needs me for a bad example anyway, with Dad and Elsa right here in the same house.

He patted her back one last time, then pushed her gently away. "Okay, Bee. I'm going to bed. You're on your own out here."

He took a step toward the door, then stopped. "Just . . . just try to stay out of trouble. All right?"

Twelve

"I t's for a good cause!" Ben shouted desperately, but it was hopeless. The hall was all but deserted for the Presidents' Day weekend, and nobody wanted his loser suckers and flowers.

"It's all right, Ben," Jenna soothed. "We didn't do that badly."

"How can you say that?" he asked, working hard to keep the quiver out of his voice. "We barely sold half of the flowers, and practically none of the suckers."

"Yeah. Good thing we bought five hundred of them," Jesse said.

Ben cringed at the criticism. "I'm sorry. I totally let you guys down."

"You did," Melanie agreed, making him feel even worse.

Nicole made a face. "Don't forget humiliated us in front of the entire school."

"I wonder if we could do anything good with the rest of these flowers," Leah mused, looking them over.

"You mean, like sell them somewhere else?" Ben asked hopefully.

"I meant like donate them to a nursing home. If we couldn't sell purple here, what makes you think we could sell it anywhere else?"

"Not to mention that they're looking a little rough since you spilled the buckets, Ben." Miguel picked up his backpack and hoisted it onto his shoulders. "I'd stay to help pick up, but I have to get to work."

"Go ahead," Ben urged, wishing he'd never had the brilliant idea of carrying all three buckets at once. "Everyone can go, in fact. I'll take care of this stuff."

Miguel nodded and took off, pausing only long enough to give Leah a quick kiss good-bye.

"What are you going to do with it all?" asked Nicole.

"I don't know," Ben admitted. "Take it home, I guess."

"When's St. Patrick's Day?" Peter asked suddenly.

"St. Patrick's Day?" Ben repeated. "What's that have to do with anything?"

But Jenna's head snapped up. "Are you thinking what I'm thinking?" she asked excitedly. A moment later she had fished a flower-covered organizer out of her backpack and was flipping through its pages. "It's on March seventeenth. That's a Wednesday this year."

"Peter, you're a genius!" Leah exclaimed.

"We can't do it here, though," Melanie said thoughtfully. "Everyone will recognize them."

"Can't do what?" Ben asked. "What are we talking about?"

"Will they keep that long?" asked Nicole.

"Sugar keeps forever," said Peter. "They'll be as good in a month as they are today."

Jesse grimaced. "That's not saying much."

"I ate one," Melanie said. "They're really not that bad. Kind of more lemon than lime."

"What are we talking about?" Ben wailed. "Why won't anyone tell me?"

"Geez, Ben. Piece it together," said Nicole. "Green suckers, St. Patrick's Day . . . this isn't rocket science."

"Oh. Right."

"Why don't Jenna and I take the suckers home?" Peter offered. "That way you'll only have to deal with the flowers."

"Sure. Go ahead." Ben crouched low over the buckets, not wanting anyone to see the tears he was blinking back. He'd ruined the sale, he'd ruined the flowers, and now Jenna and Peter didn't even trust him to keep the suckers safe.

He didn't look up as the candy was gathered back into the boxes it had come in. He heard someone snap the cash box shut, then the card table folded in front of him. Nicole and Melanie walked off with Leah and Jesse.

"Do you want us to stay and help you with the flowers?" Jenna asked.

Her voice was so full of sympathy that Ben didn't trust his to answer. He shook his head, the flowers a purple blur through his unshed tears.

Jenna and Peter hesitated, then said good-bye and walked away too, leaving him alone.

You're such a loser, Ben told himself, still staring at the buckets. All the ground he had gained with Eight Prime over the last few months, getting the group to accept him, had been lost in two short days. *And you deserve it. You have no one to blame but yourself.*

If only he'd taken an extra five minutes to read the fine print on the order form! Why did he have to be such a know-it-all?

Pulling a flower out of the water, he blinked until it swam into focus. They really didn't look as bad as Miguel had said. A few of them were broken, a few more had ripped or dirty petals, but the majority were fresh and in perfect condition. Not knowing what else to do, Ben began sorting them out, removing the bad ones and laying them on the ground, transferring the good ones into a single bucket.

Except that they didn't fit. Even subtracting the

ones they'd sold and he'd discarded, there were close to a hundred left. Ben jammed as many as he could into one bucket and sat wondering what to do with the twenty or so still remaining.

"Hey, Ben. What are you doing?" a cheerful voice asked behind him.

Ben jumped to his feet and whirled around to see Angela regarding him curiously, her backpack on her shoulders and the carnation she'd bought earlier dangling from one hand.

"Hi, Angela," he said, too embarrassed by his failure even to meet her eyes. "I'm just cleaning up these flowers."

"They left you to do this by yourself? Where's everybody else?"

"They took the table and suckers and everything. I told them I'd handle this part."

"I guess that's fair," she said dubiously, looking down at the flowers. "What are you going to do with those?"

"I don't know," he admitted. "I thought I could at least fit them into one bucket."

Seized by a sudden inspiration, he snatched the oddball twenty from the second bucket and extended them, dripping, to Angela. "Hey, do you want these?"

"Oh. Oh, no," she said, backing away with the color rushing into her cheeks. "That wouldn't be right."

"They'll just end up in the trash," he said.

"Still . . . I don't think I ought to take them."

Ben didn't need her to draw him a picture. "It doesn't mean anything, don't worry," he said, wondering how much more his ego could take. "Give them to your mom, if you want. You'll actually be helping me carry this stuff."

"But they were for charity."

"Yeah, except that's over now. If you don't take them, they'll just go to waste."

"Are you sure?" Angela asked, stretching out a tentative hand.

"Yes!" Ben pressed them on her, grateful to have finally won something, even if it was only an argument.

Adding the carnation she already held to the new bundle, she lifted them all to her nose. "They're so pretty. I can't understand why they didn't sell."

"Because they're purple. I'm a total idiot for ordering them."

"You didn't order them—they switched colors on you. Melanie told me what happened."

"Really?" Ben didn't think Melanie had even listened to his story, let alone believed it.

"People should be more flexible. So what if they aren't pink? They're pretty and they're for a good cause."

A sudden, pleased smile lit her face. Reaching into her front pants pocket, she pulled out a five-dollar bill. "I know this doesn't pay for them, but it's all I have. Take it as a contribution to the cause."

"No, Angela. I—"

"Take it," she insisted, forcing the money into his hand before she turned to leave. "I guess I'll see you Tuesday."

"Tuesday? What happened to Monday?"

"It's a three-day weekend, remember?" she asked with a laugh. "Anyway, happy Valentine's Day, Ben."

"Happy Valentine's Day," he murmured, watching her walk away.

But even being wished a happy Valentine's Day by the undisputed girl of his dreams barely penetrated his gloom. He was still Ben Pipkin, wasn't he?

How happy could his day be?

Melanie, Nicole, Leah, and Jesse walked silently across half of CCHS's front lawn before their group started to break up.

"See you guys next week," Leah said, veering off toward the left and the student parking lot.

"Yeah." Nicole took the same tack at a slightly different angle.

Melanie's bus stop was to the right, but that afternoon she kept her steps pointed straight ahead, toward the curb in front of the high school. She sped them up a little, too, to avoid being left alone with Jesse. Not that he was probably too eager to have that happen either . . .

"Aren't you catching the bus?" he startled her by asking.

She hesitated, then stopped on the wet grass. Those were the first words he'd spoken to her all week.

"I'm meeting someone," she said.

Jesse's blue eyes clouded. "Your little Hollywood boyfriend?"

"You have an active imagination, you know that? No, I'm waiting for my aunt. She's taking me to Iowa for the weekend."

"Oh." At least he had the sense to look embarrassed. "Is your mother still in town?"

"Until Monday."

"How's that going?"

"All right." He shifted his weight. "I didn't know you had an aunt in Iowa."

"Yeah, well . . . I barely know her. I'll tell you what, though—the way I'm feeling today, I wouldn't mind just staying there forever and never coming back."

She knew she sounded pathetic, but between the situation at home, the lost love staring her in the face, and the disaster she'd just endured with Eight Prime, she had never felt more hopeless. "I mean, what's the point?"

"There *is* no point," Jesse said, nodding slowly. "You ought to do it."

She stared at him, hurt and amazed. *Way to talk me out of it, Jones,* she thought bitterly.

But what had she expected? That he'd be sorry to see her go? *If it were up to him, he'd probably buy me a one-way ticket.*

"Maybe I will," she said, hoisting her heavy gym bag higher on her shoulder. "Iowa would have to be better than here."

"Anyplace is better than here."

Even though she'd more or less set him up, it still made her furious to hear him slam her home state. *Or maybe he's just implying it would be a nicer place without me in it. . . .*

A car pulled up and stopped on the street. Melanie recognized her aunt at the steering wheel.

Perfect timing! Not giving Jesse a second look, she took off across the lawn.

"See you around," he called out behind her.

She didn't even bother to answer.

"How are things going at work?" Mrs. Brewster asked unexpectedly, looking up from the grocery list she was preparing.

Nicole froze with her dinner plate halfway into the dishwasher. "Why?"

"It was nice of Mr. Roarke to let you start late today."

"Oh, yeah. He's a *real* great guy." Nicole couldn't hold back her sarcasm as she put the plate away. "We say that about him all the time."

Besides, her mother had let her borrow the car

that day, canceling out so much of the time usually wasted on the bus that Nicole had been only ten minutes late because of the Eight Prime sale—and it wasn't as if she'd been paid for it. *If Mom thinks that makes up for all the other things he does . . .*

But then, of course, her mother didn't really know anything about him.

"You ought to have more respect for your boss," Mrs. Brewster said sharply.

Nicole shrugged sullenly. *Maybe he should have more respect for us.*

"I'm going upstairs," she said, escaping to her bedroom.

But as soon as the door was closed behind her, Nicole half wished she had stayed downstairs and built on the opening her mother had given her. It might have been the best opportunity she'd ever get to confess the mess she and Gail had gotten themselves into and ask for help. Especially since the few minutes she'd managed to speak with her cousin at the restaurant that afternoon had far from reassured her that things were under control—no matter how much Gail kept insisting they were.

"Did you see him last night?" Nicole had whispered, running into Gail in the hall. She'd been on the way to get a trash bag at the time, and Gail had been carrying a mop.

"Yes." Gail's voice had been tight, her expression tense.

Assuming her cousin was afraid of being overheard, Nicole had looked over her shoulder to make sure no one else was in sight, then she'd lowered her voice even further. "How did it go?"

"Fine. It was a perfectly lovely evening."

"*What?*"

"Well, how do you think it went, Nicole? Ask another stupid question, why don't you?"

"I'm sorry," Nicole had said quickly, but her cousin's caustic words had wounded. Gail had never spoken to her that way before.

"Forget it." Gail had started to edge by with the mop, but Nicole had reached out a hand to stop her.

"Are . . . are you okay?"

Gail had tossed her head impatiently. "Of course I am. Why wouldn't I be?"

But her eyes had told a different story.

"Did he do anything to you?" Nicole had whispered nervously. "I mean, if he touched you or something—"

"Nicole, I have this under control. I said I'd handle it, and I will."

"I'm just worried about—"

"You're a little late."

Now, throwing herself onto her bed, Nicole wondered for the hundredth time what her cousin had meant by that. Was she blaming Nicole for letting her date Mr. Roarke in the first place? Or was she saying that things with their boss had gone past some point of no return? The possibility made Nicole nearly sick to her stomach. She couldn't live with herself if she thought she was responsible for something like that.

Maybe I should go back downstairs, find Mom, and spill the whole sordid story. I still could.

There was no doubt in Nicole's mind that her parents would put an end to Mr. Roarke's harassment in a hurry—or that Gail would be furious with her if she told now, after Gail had done so much to keep it secret.

Nicole twisted a handful of her bedspread, knowing she probably didn't have the courage to go against her cousin's wishes and tell on Mr. Roarke anyway. Besides, would anyone believe her if she did?

And there was something else, of course—perhaps the biggest fear of all. If she did tell, what would happen to *her*?

Thirteen

"Hey, Dad?" Ben poked his head into the dim downstairs study, where his father was already up and hard at work designing another computer game. "Can I talk to you about something?"

"Yeah, come on in," his father replied, never lifting his eyes from a huge color monitor. "You've got to see this jujitsu gopher I just put in. He's really cool."

"A jujitsu what?" Ben walked around behind his father. On the computer screen, a furry brown rodent leveled one opponent with a mad flurry of paralyzing blows, then did back handsprings into another.

"Never mind. But, uh, what do gophers have to do with space travel?" The last Ben had heard, his father's new game was an Apollo 13–style adventure involving astronauts in danger.

"This is part of the dream sequence," his father explained, totally absorbed by his creation. "For when the astronauts' oxygen starts to run out."

"Remind me never to be an astronaut."

"At least not on one of my spaceships," his father chortled. The gopher cartwheeled off the screen. "So, what's up, Ben? You doing anything fun today to start off the three-day weekend?"

"I might go over to Mark's house later. But that isn't what I wanted to ask you."

"Oh?" Mr. Pipkin finally tore his eyes away from his work.

"You know all those flowers I brought home last night?"

"The ones stuffing vases all over the house? No. I hadn't noticed."

"At least Mom liked them," Ben said glumly.

"Are you kidding me? She loved them."

"Yeah, but no one else did. And they were supposed to help us earn money for the Junior Explorers."

"I know it's disappointing," his father said, finally becoming serious, "but don't be too hard on yourself. It's not your fault they sent you the wrong things. If you want my opinion, the whole transaction was pretty shady."

"Shady how?"

"They must have known you didn't want two hundred purple flowers. I mean, you didn't *order* purple. You asked for a bunch of Valentine's colors with a Valentine's delivery. I'm guessing they ran out of the popular colors and pulled a fast one on you."

"Even if you're right, I'm the idiot who picked

that shady company. Everyone trusted me, and I let them down," Ben said with a sigh.

"And what do you want to do about it? Do you want me to help you write a letter of complaint? Because if you want to fight this, I'll help however I can."

"It's too late. If I was going to fight them, I should have started when the boxes arrived, not three days later."

"That would have been better. But it's still not hopeless if—"

"I just want to forget this ever happened, Dad. And the only way I can do that is to make it up to Eight Prime. I was hoping you'd lend me the money for the flowers that didn't sell, so I can pay my friends back. I'll work it off in extra chores or any way you want."

"You shouldn't have to do that, Ben. Holding that sale was a group venture, and losing money was a risk you all took together."

"Not really, because I talked everyone else into it—not to mention into using their own money. Please, Dad. I was the captain of this *Titanic*. It's my duty to sink with the ship."

"Do the other kids even *want* you to pay them back?" Mr. Pipkin asked. "I don't think that's very nice."

"No, it's what *I* want, Dad. Please. I have to."

Reluctantly Ben's father took his wallet from his

back pocket and removed a blank check from among the bills. Smoothing it flat on the desk, he picked up a pen. "I want you to know that this isn't about the money, Ben. I don't mind losing a few bucks, I just don't think your friends—"

"I know what I'm doing, Dad. Really."

Mr. Pipkin sighed. "How much should I write it for?"

Jesse tried to ignore the kitchen-counter conversation between his father and Elsa while he ate his breakfast at the nearby table, but every word they said just drew him in further.

"I can't understand why she isn't up yet," Elsa complained to her husband. Ripping open another packet, she stirred Sweet'n Low into her fourth cup of coffee. "Brittany used to be so cheerful in the morning, and the last couple of days I can barely drag her out of bed."

A hangover will do that, Jesse thought, hoping it was just depression. Either way, there was no chance he was jumping into this conversation—not after he'd promised the little brat he wouldn't tell unless he caught her drinking again. Besides, he was leaving to meet his mother in fifteen minutes; he didn't need any complications. He shoveled in cereal a little faster, wishing he were already gone.

"Who cares how long she sleeps?" Dr. Jones said, still trying to read the newspaper he'd spread on the counter. "It's Saturday. Let her sleep all day if it keeps her out of our hair."

"It's not good," Elsa insisted. "It just makes her that much harder to get moving on school days."

"Then go get her out of bed," he said irritably. "Why are you involving me in such trivia?"

"I thought you might care."

Dr. Jones flipped a page. "Apparently not."

Elsa gave her husband a frosty look, then put her coffee cup down and stalked out of the kitchen. Jesse began eating even faster, eager to avoid talking to his father now that they were the only two people in the room.

He needn't have worried. Freed from the distraction of his wife, Dr. Jones became completely immersed in his reading. Nothing broke the silence until Elsa screamed.

"Clint! Clint, come quick!"

Her voice sounded frantic. Jesse and his father exchanged panicked glances, then bolted for the stairs. Elsa was already running down, and everyone met on the landing.

"Look!" she cried, waving a crumpled scrap of paper at them. "Brittany's run away!"

"That's ridiculous." Dr. Jones snatched the note from her hand. "Where could she possibly go?"

Tears streaked Elsa's pale cheeks. "I don't know. Oh, God, I don't even know when she left. It could have been anytime last night."

"Okay, we have to stay calm," said her husband. "Get her address book and start calling all her friends. Jesse, you get a picture of her and drive around to the places kids hang out. The park, the movies—you'll know better than I do. Ask if anybody's seen her. I'll go check the buses and trains."

"Where would she go on a train?" Elsa demanded shakily. "That's crazy."

"This whole thing is crazy! Do you have a better idea?"

Elsa opened her mouth, then shut it hard. Spinning around, she ran back upstairs, presumably to make the calls.

"Get a photo and go," Dr. Jones told Jesse before he followed his wife up the stairs.

Jesse turned and raced in the other direction, pausing only long enough to grab one of Brittany's pictures off the stairwell wall before he skidded through the entry on his way to the garage.

He was in his car and halfway down the street before he remembered he was supposed to be meeting his mother. He hadn't even called her.

She'll call the house when I don't show up, he reassured himself. *Or maybe I can find a pay phone*.

It wasn't as if he had any choice about looking for Brittany, so his mother would have to forgive him. How could he *not* help look for her with everyone in such a panic?

Not that she probably got too far. She's only twelve.

171

Which, now that he thought about it, made things kind of scarier. He thought of the countless stories he'd heard about stalkers who preyed on innocent young girls. And how young and innocent Brittany really was . . .

No wonder Elsa was terrified.

"For Pete's sake, Bee!" he shouted, as if she could hear him. "You're only twelve!"

"Gail's dating *who*?" Mrs. Brewster screeched.

"I knew you were going to freak out," moaned Nicole, wringing her hands. "I never should have told you."

"You're telling me that Gail—little Gail—is going out with your thirty-four-year-old boss." Mr. Brewster's voice was much calmer, and therefore much scarier, than his wife's as he leaned toward Nicole across the dining room table, ignoring the sandwich in front of him.

"Yes, but she doesn't *want* to," Nicole tried to explain. "For one thing, she has a boyfriend, and he's much closer to her age—only nineteen or twenty."

"Does her mother know all this?" Mrs. Brewster demanded.

Too late, Nicole realized she shouldn't have mentioned Neil. *I shouldn't have mentioned any of it. What was I thinking?*

The three of them were all eating lunch at home that Saturday, with Heather off at a friend's house.

172

Nicole hadn't planned to tell on Gail, but the problem with Mr. Roarke had gradually become the top thing on her mind. When her father had asked about her job, the self-satisfied smile on his face saying how well he assumed it was going, Nicole found that she couldn't keep quiet any longer. Now, having blundered onto the course she'd tried for so long to avoid, she blurted out the whole story.

"Gail didn't even do anything that bad. I mean, she shouldn't have given that guy free food, but she's a good worker and Mr. Roarke's rules are so stupid. It's not her fault if—"

"Gail stole food?" Mr. Brewster roared.

"Well, I . . . kind of. But it was only a couple of dollars' worth." The hamburgers and hot dogs Gail had snuck to Neil's car on a previous occasion immediately sprang to mind, but Nicole shut her eyes, squeezing out the memory.

"And then Mr. Roarke said if she went out with him he'd take care of everything. But we thought he only meant once, and now he's getting all these weird ideas and—"

"Go to your room," her father said, cutting her off.

"But—"

"*Now*, Nicole!"

She could hear him already on the phone to his brother as she ran up the stairs to her bedroom.

"Dan? It's Jim. Listen, I'm sorry to have to tell you this, but we've got a big problem."

Nicole hesitated at her door, tempted to eavesdrop, then slammed it instead. She wasn't going to hear anything she didn't already know. Her dad would tell his brother everything, Uncle Dan would call his friend who owned the restaurant, Mr. Roarke would find out Nicole had told on him, and Gail would hate her forever. She and Gail would lose their jobs, because there was no way Mr. Roarke would let them stay now. And sooner or later, when her parents had had a little more time to think, Nicole would be punished for her silent complicity in Gail's crimes.

Throwing herself down on her bed, she cried from a full heart.

And I was afraid they wouldn't believe me. It would have been better if they hadn't!

"You haven't seen her?" Jesse persisted, pushing Brittany's picture forward more insistently. "You're sure?"

"Dude! I already told you no. Anyway, a girl like that could have walked right by without me noticing. She's kind of young for you, isn't she?"

"She's my sister, you moron." Jesse's free hand formed a fist at his side. It would be so easy to start a fight with this total stranger, if only to take his mind off his fear.

The other guy gave him a scornful look, then turned and walked away from the corner, making

Jesse's decision for him. He hesitated only a second, then ran back to his BMW. He didn't have time for distractions.

Tossing Brittany's picture into the passenger seat, Jesse climbed into his car and pulled back onto the pavement—an act he'd already performed so many times he'd lost count. He'd been searching for hours, and he was out of places to look. No one had seen Brittany anywhere.

I guess I could go home and see if there's any news there, he thought.

But he had been to the house at lunchtime, a couple of hours before, and the scene had been even worse than when he'd first left. Elsa had called every number she could think of, all to no avail, and Dr. Jones's search of the bus and train stations had come up dry too. Jesse had called his mother to cancel their plans, even though she'd already spoken to Elsa. Dr. Jones had called the police and then, before the officers could arrive, Elsa had sent her husband back out to check the grounds at Sacred Heart and comb the local mall.

I wish I could have been there to see that.

Jesse made a random left turn, his eyes restlessly scanning the residential sidewalks as he tried to imagine his father in the Saturday crowds at the mall. Dr. Jones hated to shop at places he considered beneath his dignity. The thought of him checking all the girls' stores and teen departments, stopping women with packs of toddlers just to show them Brittany's picture, was almost as amazing to Jesse as Brittany's leaving in the first place. Even so, his father hadn't hesitated to go, and Jesse had no doubt that the mall was being searched with the same military efficiency his father brought to everything else.

"Which means he's accomplishing more than I am." Glancing at the clock on his dashboard, Jesse decided to stop at a pay phone. He wasn't doing any good just driving around anyway.

Elsa snatched up his call on the first ring. "Hello?" she cried, her desperate voice conveying the situation in one word.

"It's Jesse. I guess you didn't find her yet."

"Has anybody seen her?"

"No, and I've been everywhere. I don't know what more I can do."

"Please, Jesse, don't give up. I can't bear not knowing where she is, and the police won't search until she's been missing longer. You and your dad are my only hope."

"She's probably just at a friend's house. How far can she have gotten?"

"She's not! I called them all—even the girls she doesn't like anymore." There were tears in Elsa's voice now. "You have to find her, Jesse."

"But . . . do you have any idea where I should look?"

"Look all over. You know where better than I do. Please."

"I guess I could keep driving around."

"Thank you, Jesse. I won't forget this."

Jesse hung up the phone at a loss. He didn't know where to look next, but he knew he had to look somewhere. Hadn't he just promised Elsa he would? He didn't even know why he had, except that his stepmother had never spoken to him that way before. She had treated him like . . . like . . .

Like an adult, he thought with amazement.

She hadn't ordered him to help, she had begged him to. She hadn't told him where to look, she had trusted his judgment. Weirdest of all, she had seemed to be relying on some sort of unspoken connection between them—one Jesse had never known she felt.

"Okay, think," he ordered himself, climbing into his car once more. "If *I* ran away, where would I go?"

The answer was obvious: straight out of town. He'd point his car toward the interstate and drive without looking back.

Brittany was too young to drive, though, and so were all her friends. She'd have had to take a bus or a train, and Dr. Jones had made sure that no one had sold her a ticket and now nobody would. She had no way to leave.

Unless she walked.

Which wasn't even possible. There hadn't been

any snow yet that week, but it wasn't exactly balmy, either. Skinny Brittany would freeze in a couple of hours when the sun went down.

Unless she hitchhiked.

Jesse forgot to breathe. She wouldn't be that stupid. Would she? Growing up in California, she had to know that was a sure way to end up dead.

Except that they weren't in California anymore. And things in Clearwater Crossing seemed so different. So much safer . . .

Wrenching the key in the ignition, Jesse roared away from the curb. A person could stand around hitchhiking anywhere, of course, but for someone trying to get out of town, there was one really obvious place. He pointed his car toward it now, praying as the downtown streets slipped by.

On the far side of town, past the warehouses and railroad tracks, the few streets that remained funneled to a V pointing straight at the freeway. The V became an on-ramp, and just before the ramp merged into traffic, a gravel turnout allowed for last-minute stops. Jesse strained to see if anyone was standing there and thought he caught a flash of white disappearing into the bushes. Gravel spat from beneath his tires as he pulled off the pavement, breaking to a hasty stop in the turnout.

"Brittany!" he shouted, jumping out of the car. "Brittany, I know you're in there. I saw you."

He was pretty sure he'd seen something, anyway. But when Brittany actually emerged from the bushes he could barely believe his eyes. Her face was a tear-streaked mess, her hair was full of twigs, her shoulders bowed beneath an overstuffed backpack, and from one hand dangled a white cardboard sign with the letters CA in heavy black marker.

"What are you doing here, Jesse?" she asked accusingly, tears rolling down her cheeks. "I'm not going home."

"Oh yes you are." Pulling the sign from her hand, he threw it to the ground. "Are you crazy? What are you thinking?"

She was sobbing so hard she could barely speak. "You're leaving—why shouldn't I?"

"You mean with my mom?" he asked incredulously. "How can you even compare the two things? At least I have a place to go."

The right hook Brittany threw at his face was so vicious and so unexpected that he barely ducked in time.

"You think you're so great just because you have two parents!" she shouted, half blinded by her own tears. "Well, I have two parents too. I just don't . . . don't . . ."

Know who one of them is, Jesse finished for her, feeling like the biggest jerk in the world.

How could he have been so dense? Brittany's

mouthing off, her recent wild behavior . . . it all seemed so obvious now. She was jealous because his mom was in town.

I've been an idiot not to see it.

His little stepsister had always acted so pleased with her life, so admiring of her stuck-up mother, and so incredibly in love with herself. He realized now he'd had no idea how deeply unhappy she was. For all he knew, maybe she'd never wanted her mom to marry his dad in the first place. Maybe leaving Malibu for Missouri wasn't her idea of a good trade either. Maybe she felt as crushed and overwhelmed as he did by the sheer number of days until she'd be free. Maybe she missed her old home, her school, her friends, the girl she used to be. . . .

And Jesse could really relate to that type of pain.

"Listen, Bee," he said, putting out a cautious hand. He kept his weight on his toes, ready to dodge if she made a fist. "I'm not going anywhere. I know things at home have been pretty bad lately, but they're going to get better. I promise."

She seemed past hearing as she stood there sobbing, immobilized by her grief. Stripping her heavy pack from her shoulders, he coaxed her into his car and put her things in the back. She faced stubbornly straight ahead, still crying, forcing him to buckle her seat belt for her.

But her tears began to die down as he turned the BMW toward home.

"You promise you're not leaving?" she asked.

"I said I'm staying."

At least for now. If nothing else, could he really leave Melanie without trying one more time?

That's assuming she's coming back from Iowa. But she must be. Right? She couldn't have been serious about staying.

Jesse's neck and shoulders were tight from gripping the wheel for so many hours. His head throbbed from the stress. Putting a tired hand to his temples, he squeezed them as he drove.

What a day, he thought, feeling completely, totally drained. *I could really use a drink.*

Fourteen

"Did you have fun walking the dogs?" Sarah asked sulkily.

Surprised, Jenna stopped in the still-dark den, only to spot her youngest sister glaring at her from beneath a pile of blankets on the sofa.

"Sarah! Shouldn't you be getting ready for church, or breakfast, or . . . something?" Jenna asked, flustered. "Mom's going to be serving any second, and you know how she gets when we're late."

Sarah swung her legs to the floor, then tossed an unopened book and her blankets aside. "I'm already dressed," she said, gesturing from her Sunday best to Jenna's wet jeans and boots. "And since Mom's making strawberry waffles for Valentine's Day, you're the one who'd better hurry."

"Uh-oh. Thanks for the tip."

Their mom was annoyed by latecomers under any circumstances—more so on Sundays, when conducting their church choir made her schedule especially tight. But on a Sunday morning when she was also cooking a special breakfast . . .

"I'd better go tell Caitlin," Jenna said, glancing nervously back toward the garage. "She's still out there fooling around with Abby."

She turned, but before she could leave the room, Sarah got off the couch and blocked her path.

"Jenna, why don't you like me anymore?" she asked.

"What? Of course I like you!"

"Then why don't you want me around? Why can't I do anything with you and Caitlin?"

"Who said you can't do stuff with us? Just because I didn't want you to walk the dogs last week—"

"Or this week."

"You didn't ask this week! I'm not a mind reader."

Sarah made a face. "I'm not going to beg two weeks in a row. You could have asked me."

"Look, Sarah, you never even mentioned it. And anyway, I honestly don't know why you're so hot on going. It's cold and wet and—"

"I just want to do something with someone! Everyone's got a best friend here but me. Mom has Dad, Maggie has Allison, you have Caitlin, and who do I have? No one! Ever since you changed all the rooms around, I'm the only person in the family who has to live alone."

"*What?*" Jenna barely knew where to start. True, her plan to swap the girls' bedrooms had unexpectedly ended with Sarah getting one to herself, but Jenna couldn't believe her sister was actually upset about a situation anyone else would have loved—or that Sarah could seriously suggest she was living alone in a household with six other people. "That's crazy, Sarah. No one has special friends here. We're a family."

"It doesn't seem like it," Sarah said grouchily.

"Look, I'd sit with you at church today except I have to sing. But after church . . . well, no. Today's not good. But maybe tomorrow . . ." Although she really didn't see herself spending Presidents' Day with her sister either, when she could be doing something with Peter.

She glanced toward the garage again, hoping for all their sakes that Caitlin was hurrying. "Or next weekend for sure. I'll talk to Caitlin, and if we don't all walk the dogs we'll do something else. Go to a movie, maybe."

"Do you *promise*?" Sarah asked, a tentative smile creeping onto her face.

"Sure, if nothing comes up. I still don't know why you want to hang out with us, though, when you could play with friends your own age."

The garage door opened before Sarah could answer. Caitlin walked into the house, a freshly toweled Abby trotting along behind her.

"We have to hurry and get dressed," Jenna said. "Mom's making Valentine's waffles."

Caitlin raised her eyebrows and ran for the stairs.

"I'm going up now too," Jenna told Sarah. "The last thing I need today is to make Mom mad at me."

Not with my big date with Peter tonight.

I can't wait! she thought for the millionth time as she bounded up the stairway, the smell of sausage filling her nostrils. Her new dress was already hanging on the closet door. Her presents for Peter were wrapped and ready to go. All that remained was to wait until evening to see what romantic plan Peter had cooked up for their first Valentine's Day together.

Or maybe I can get him to tell me after church, she thought, ever hopeful. *He can't keep me in the dark forever!*

"Hello, Mrs. Altmann," said Ben. "Is Peter home?"

"Come on in, Ben," she said, motioning him through the Altmanns' front door and toward the living room. "Why don't you sit down, and I'll just go tell him you're here?"

Peter arrived a few seconds later, a bemused smile on his face. "Hi, Ben. I didn't expect to see you today."

"Is this a bad time?" Ben asked, jumping out of his chair. "I mean, you're not about to eat dinner or anything?"

"Not for a couple of hours," said Peter, shaking his head. His dark blond hair was wet, as if he'd just come from the shower. "So what are you doing here? Just cruising the neighborhood?"

"No, I brought you something important."

Reaching into his pocket, Ben removed the folded check his father had given him the day before. "I've got the money for the flowers," he said, handing it over. "I was going to wait and bring it to school, but with the long weekend and everything . . ."

He took a deep breath. "I just wanted everyone to know I was paying them back."

"What?" Far from the delight Ben had anticipated, Peter looked almost angry. "Who told you you had to pay us back?"

"No one. I want to."

"But, Ben, how come? We all lost that money together. Everyone knows it wasn't your fault."

His friend was starting to sound suspiciously like his father, but Ben stubbornly held his ground. "I don't think they do. Besides, it *was* my fault. The suckers we can still make up, but I won't be able to look the group in the eye until I pay for those flowers."

Grabbing Peter's hand, Ben forced the check into it. "You have to take it."

"All right," Peter finally agreed. "I'll use it to pay the others back. But once we have money in the account again, I'm paying you back too. We're all in this together."

"We can talk about it then," Ben said, pleased

with the manly way he'd handled things. By Tuesday afternoon everyone in Eight Prime would know that Ben Pipkin took care of his friends.

Peter put the check in his pocket.

"So do you want to hang out?" Ben asked happily.

"You mean, tomorrow?" Peter asked, his brows bunched with confusion.

"No, right now. We could go over to The Danger Zone and play a few rounds of Maniac Marauders. We could even order a pizza or something."

"Sorry, Ben. It's Valentine's Day, remember? I have a date with Jenna."

"Oh. Right."

If he had felt like a man for an instant, it only made him more aware of what a stupid little boy he was. Only a loser like him could forget the most romantic day of the year.

Of course everyone has dates tonight. Everyone but me, that is.

So much for feeling good about himself. Suddenly all he could think of was the fact that he'd never been out with anyone. Not on Valentine's Day, not on any day. Not unless he counted that movie with Mary Alwin way back in junior high.

You'd better *count it*, he told himself, heading for the Altmanns' front door. *At this rate it's likely to be the only date you ever have.*

* * *

Nicole jumped nervously when the phone rang, at a loss to guess who'd be calling. Courtney was at the movies with Emily that night, both of them pretending that hanging out together was more fun than a Valentine's date. Nicole saw through that lie, of course, but she still would have liked to go with them. Instead, her parents were out on a dinner date, and Nicole was stuck home in disgrace, supposedly keeping an eye on Heather.

"Although, perhaps Heather should baby-sit *you*," had been her mother's parting shot. "She seems to have more sense."

The phone shrilled again. Rolling over the magazines scattered across her bed, Nicole snatched it off the nightstand. "Hello?"

"Thanks a lot, Nicole!" a voice sobbed over the line. "You've completely ruined my life!"

"Gail?" Nicole guessed.

"How could you do this to me? Especially after what I've been through. I told you I had things under control!"

Nicole felt sick, but she knew she owed her cousin an explanation. "I just . . . I don't trust Mr. Roarke. And I was really afraid for you, Gail. I was afraid he was going to hurt you."

"So you decided to do the job for him? If this is how you treat your friends, I'd hate to be your enemy!"

"I'm sorry, Gail. You can't imagine how I wish that none of this ever happened."

The only reply was the sound of Gail practically choking on her tears.

"If it's any consolation, I'm in just as much trouble as you are," Nicole added desperately. "I mean, we're both sure to be fired now."

"Ju—Just as much trouble?" Gail sputtered. "Is that what you think? Listen, Nicole, the owner fired two people all right: me and Mr. Roarke. You get to keep your job."

"Are you kidding?" Nicole wailed. "I don't even *want* that job!"

"Is that why you told? To get yourself fired? Thanks for taking me down with you!"

"No, I did it for you, Gail. I swear. I was only trying to help."

"Why did you tell your parents about Neil, then? Was that supposed to help me too?"

Nicole's heart sank, weighed down by her own guilt. "That just sort of slipped out. I'm really sorry."

"So what?" Gail cried. "You're really sorry, and I'm never allowed to see my boyfriend again. That's fair, right? You're being punished as much as I am."

"No, Gail," said Nicole, frantic to make her understand. "I really thought—"

"I told you I was *handling* it!" Gail sobbed into the phone.

The line went dead. Gail had hung up.

"Great," Nicole whimpered, tears starting to match her cousin's. "I'm such an idiot!"

Why couldn't she have left things alone, the way Gail had begged her to? What business was it of hers if her cousin dated Mr. Roarke?

Instead I had to open my big mouth.

Now her parents were mad at her, Gail thought she was a horrible person, and she'd gotten two people fired.

Nicole hid her face in a pillow as her tears turned into sobs. *Everybody hates me, and I still have to work at Wienerageous!*

"After you," Peter said with a smile, opening the restaurant's carved wooden door and gesturing Jenna through it.

Jenna slipped past him into the luxurious interior, feeling like a queen. The night had barely begun, and it was already the best of her life.

Peter had picked her up in his mother's car, which had been washed spotless for the occasion; put a silver bracelet on her wrist; and presented her with a single, long-stemmed red rose. The flower made the perfect accent to the dark pink of her new dress, which exactly complemented Peter's navy blue suit. Thrilled, she'd given him a homemade card covered with hearts and kisses, a bright red baseball cap, and a book: *How to Start and Run Your Own Summer Day*

Camp. Not the most romantic title, perhaps, but by the excitement in his eyes, she'd known she'd picked just right. Now, her gaze on the candlelit tables before her, she brought the rose up to her face as Peter lifted her sweater from her shoulders, handing it to an attendant by the door.

"Le Papillon," she whispered, barely able to believe she was finally going to eat there. "Perfect."

"Altmann, party of two," Peter announced to the tuxedoed maitre d'.

The next thing Jenna knew, they were being shown between white-draped tables heavy with china and silver to an intimate corner table for two. Candles glowed from the floral centerpieces and sconces on the walls, their light augmented by the chandeliers dripping crystal overhead. Everywhere she turned, elegant couples made quiet conversation or sampled the elaborate cuisine. Jenna had never felt more grown up.

"Let me get your chair," Peter said, rushing to pull it out for her.

She stifled a giggle as she walked to her seat. She and Peter in a fancy restaurant, acting so formal with each other, was not a scenario she could have imagined even a few short months ago. But now she let her head brush his shoulder as she sat down, wanting that whisper of contact. Peter drew a deep breath, inhaling the hint of perfume she was wearing. Then he took his own chair, and they faced each other across the table, Jenna full of excitement about the changes in their relationship and the possibilities for their future.

"Are Caitlin and David coming here too?" she asked, hoping so for her sister's sake. David had whisked Caitlin away in the Toyota before Peter had arrived, and of course Caitlin hadn't bothered to ask him where they were going, leaving Jenna in the dark regarding their plans.

"No. They're going to Harry's," said Peter, naming a local steak house.

"Harry's is nice."

Not Le Papillon nice, she added to herself. But still, a good choice for a first date. She couldn't wait to hear all about it later that night.

"I'm so happy those two got together. Aren't you?" Jenna asked, opening a menu bound in burgundy leather with a single gold butterfly on the front. "It looked bad there for a while, but everything worked out perfectly."

"See?" Peter teased. "Sometimes things go well even *without* your help."

"That's what you think," Jenna retorted. "I was plenty of help."

"If you say so," he replied with a mischievous grin.

"I'll tell you what, though," she confided, scanning a list of fancy appetizers. "There was a time when I didn't have much hope for that relationship. I was really afraid Caitlin was going to blow it and lose David to Mary Beth, the way I almost did when Melanie liked you."

"What are you talking about?" Peter asked incredulously. "David was never even interested in Mary Beth."

"Sure. We know that *now*."

"And when did Melanie like me? We're just friends."

"She asked you to the homecoming dance."

"Yes, but I was in love with you the whole time."

He couldn't have said a more perfect thing. Jenna lowered her menu, a sudden lump in her throat. "Really? That's so sweet."

"It's just the truth," he said, turning red. "I was thinking of you every minute of that dance."

"You were?"

"Of course! Even that time she kissed me, I—"

Jenna's menu dropped to the table, knocking over a full water glass. Heads turned, but she barely noticed. Her heart pumped. Her cheeks burned. She couldn't catch her breath.

"Even that time she *what?*"

"No, watch this!" Kathy cried, throwing a piece of popcorn into the air. Without leaving her barstool, she dodged her head under the falling kernel, caught it in her mouth, and clapped her hands in front of her chest, making noises like a seal.

"Nice," said Melanie, laughing on the next stool. "Very attractive."

"Your aunt started it." Kathy pointed across the counter at Gwen, who was heating a pan of milk on the stove.

Gwen smiled, reached into her bathrobe pocket, and threw three M&M's in the air, catching them in sequence as they cascaded down to her mouth.

"The first, and still the best . . . Ms. Gwen Allen!" she declared, taking a bow.

"You're crazy," Melanie teased her. "Don't you know you're supposed to be setting an example?"

"I'm doing my best, but you girls are barely trying. If you want to be any good, you have to practice." Gwen threw another candy into the air, spinning around to catch it backward.

Melanie could barely believe she was hanging out with an adult, the way her aunt fit in with her and Kathy. That weekend, now that the newness of knowing each other was wearing off, Aunt Gwen had really loosened up, behaving more like a friend than a relative. Melanie had known adults who tried so hard to be one of the kids that they only embarrassed themselves—not to mention everyone else—but Gwen wasn't that way at all. She didn't slaughter the newest slang, or tell lame stories about the not-so-cool high jinks she'd gotten up to when she was a kid. She was just . . . still young.

"This is better than having dates," Kathy declared, helping herself to a handful of M&M's from the bowl on the counter. "Going out on Valentine's Day is too much pressure unless you really like the guy."

"I agree," said Melanie. "Going out is too much pressure in general."

Although she couldn't help wondering what Jesse was doing that night. Did he have a date? Who with? Or would he be hanging out with his mother? He couldn't exactly ditch her on her last weekend in town, even if it was Valentine's Day.

I'll bet he's with his mother, she thought, wishing she didn't care.

Aunt Gwen took the milk off the stove and poured it into three mugs filled with chocolate, stirring each in turn, then squirting on blobs of whipped cream. "This ought to put us to sleep," she said, passing two of them across the counter. "I don't know what it is about hot milk, but it always knocks me out."

"I have to go soon anyway," Kathy said, checking her watch. "That movie we rented was *long*. I'm glad I saw it here instead of in a theater, where you can't even stretch out your legs."

"Yeah, or pause it every fifteen minutes to use the bathroom," Melanie teased.

"I drink a lot of water! It's supposed to be good for your skin."

Melanie slurped some of the melted cream from her mug. "I wish hot chocolate was good for the skin. I could drink this five times a day."

"Me too," said Aunt Gwen. "You must have gotten that gene from my side of the family."

"Um, yeah," Melanie said uncomfortably. "Maybe."

"Where did I get it from, then?" Kathy wondered. "I love chocolate more than anything."

"That's one bad thing about not having a date for Valentine's Day," Gwen said. "No heart-shaped boxes of chocolate."

"Don't even *speak* to me about heart-shaped boxes of chocolate," Melanie groaned. From what she'd heard, the student council had sold out of their stock by noon on the second day.

"Yeah. No one ever gave me one either," said Kathy, misunderstanding.

The three of them sipped their drinks in silence after that, lost in their separate thoughts, until Kathy slid off her stool.

"Well, I'd better get going," she said, reluctantly crossing the room to take her coat off the hook by the door. "What time are you leaving tomorrow, Melanie?"

Melanie looked to her aunt.

"Sometime in the morning. Not too early," said Gwen.

"I'll try to catch you before you go." Pulling a fur-lined hood over her short hair, Kathy waved before she opened the door and slipped out into the snowy night.

"I don't know about you, but I'm about ready for bed," Gwen said. "I want to give you something first, though."

Melanie watched curiously as her aunt opened the glass-fronted door of a china cupboard and carefully removed a softball-sized wad of tissue.

"I think this is yours," she said, setting it on the counter.

Mystified, Melanie reached for the crumpled ball and began unwinding its layers. But when the object in the center was revealed, she stared at it uncomprehendingly. How had Aunt Gwen gotten the angel ornament Melanie had left on her mother's grave?

"It probably seemed like I wrote to you out of the blue," Gwen said, brushing a gentle finger across the angel's golden hair. "But it wasn't exactly that way. You see, I found her first."

"But how?"

Melanie had buried the tiny figure in the snow in front of her mother's headstone on Christmas Eve. No one could have seen it there. And even if there had been a thaw or something, what had made her aunt so certain Melanie had been the one who'd hidden it?

"When you came to town to go to the cemetery that day, you stopped at a restaurant to ask a waitress for directions. Remember?" Aunt Gwen said.

"Vaguely." Melanie and Jesse had been arguing because she'd forgotten the map. Desperate to keep him from turning and driving straight back to Clearwater Crossing, she'd ducked into a restaurant to ask for help.

"Well, that waitress went to school with your mom. It took her a couple of days to figure out why seeing you gave her such a déjà vu, but when she finally did she called me to ask if Tristyn's daughter had been in town. I always knew you'd show up sometime, to see your mother's grave. And when I went out there myself, something just told me to clear the snow."

Aunt Gwen lifted the ornament by its loop of gold thread, and they both watched it spin in a slow circle. "Look. Not a scratch on it," she said, handing the thread to Melanie.

Melanie took it reluctantly, a tiny part of her past she thought she'd finally put behind her.

"You should keep that," said her aunt. "I know your mom would want you to have it."

"All right," Melanie said, lowering it into the paper. She didn't really want it, but she didn't want to hurt her aunt's feelings, either.

"Aunt Gwen," she burst out impulsively. "What happened? I mean with my mom. What made her leave here? And why didn't any of you talk after that?"

Aunt Gwen drew back, surprised by the question. "You mean you still don't know?"

Melanie shook her head. "Mom never talked about things like that."

"Well, I guess I could . . ." Her aunt rubbed one cheek distractedly. "But it would probably be better if you talked to your father. Yes, I think you ought to ask him."

Yeah, right, thought Melanie, rolling her eyes. *There isn't anything I want to know that bad.*

Fifteen

"So, I guess this is it," Jesse's mother said, hesitating beside her rental car in the hotel parking lot.

Jesse nodded. "I'll miss you."

"You're sure you want to stay?"

"It's better. For now. I didn't think there was anything here, but . . . the last few days have made me realize some things."

Stepping forward, his mother wrapped him in a hug. "It *is* better. I'll miss you too, but you can't pack up and move every time you have a problem. Besides, you'll be going off to college soon, and another transfer isn't likely to help your transcript."

Jesse nodded, knowing he ought to care more about that. Instead he found himself thinking about the people he'd met in Missouri.

"True. Not to mention that this charity group I joined is in a bind right now. I should probably help them out."

He didn't mention Melanie—he never had—but she was the real reason he couldn't bail on Eight

Prime. Whatever was going on—or not going on—between them wasn't finished yet. He needed to stay until it was.

And then, of course, there was Brittany. . . .

"You don't have to apologize," his mother said, letting him go and wiping her eyes. "I understand."

"We have a week off for spring break pretty soon. Maybe I could come visit you."

"We might be able to swing that."

"Do you think Kevin and Steve could come too? We could have a reunion or something."

No one could accuse him of desertion if he was gone only a week, and he could get into hitting the beach with his brothers again, surfing and scoping out the girls in their spring-break bikinis.

His mother looked less thrilled by the idea than he was. "I don't live in a big house anymore, Jesse. Having four of us crowded into my two-bedroom condo would probably get pretty old before the week was over."

"No, it would be fun. We'd be outside most of the time anyway, and I don't mind sleeping in the living room."

"Well, we'll have to see. I'll call your brothers and find out what they're doing."

"All right." This time it was Jesse who hugged her. "Thanks for coming to see me."

The words sounded strange, but he didn't know

what else to say. For a week the two of them had been mother and son again—now they were resuming their separate lives.

"It won't be so long this time," she promised, reading his mind. "I'm going to call more often."

Both of them had tears in their eyes as she climbed into her car and he kissed her cheek through the open window. "Drive safe," he said.

"You too."

"I'm not driving anywhere."

"Well, you know. In general."

"All right."

He watched her drive off into a gathering storm, wondering if she'd hit snow. *Even if she does, she'll only be in it until she flies out. I'm the one who's stuck here.*

Still, wasn't that exactly what he'd just said he wanted?

It won't be that bad. And if it is, I'll just change my mind.

Nicole stepped through her front door and looked down at the torn envelope in her hands, feeling completely discouraged. Wienerageous paid its employees every other Monday, and she had just returned from picking up her first measly paycheck, sneaking in through the back door to grab it unobserved.

Now I know how they can pay us on a holiday, she

thought unhappily. There was a two-week gap between that Monday and the last day she'd been paid for—a built-in slowdown that allowed an accountant to write all the checks in advance. As a result, her paycheck was for only half the amount she'd expected.

Less than half, she corrected herself, *because they took out all those deductions*.

"Did you put gas in the car like I asked you to?" her mother called from the kitchen.

Sighing, Nicole walked in to join her. "Yes. Here."

Barely looking her in the face, Nicole handed her mother the car keys and the envelope.

"What's this?" Mrs. Brewster asked, pulling out the check.

"About half of what I owe you for that vase. I thought I'd have it all, but the way they do the checks . . ."

She shook her head, too choked up to explain. It was just so depressing to work so hard for so little. *No wonder Mom was mad when I broke the stupid thing*, she thought. *I had absolutely no idea what it was worth*.

"A lot of places pay this way," her mother said. "It's pretty standard."

"Yeah, well. In two more weeks I should have the rest of it. I'm . . . I'm sorry," she added haltingly.

Feeling the tears about to start again, she turned to leave the room.

"Nicole, wait." Standing quickly, her mother stopped her with a hand on her shoulder. "I'm sorry too."

"*You're* sorry? What for?"

"I was so worried when you told me about the situation at work that I'm afraid I overreacted. You should have told us sooner, and we were angry that you didn't. But I've been thinking about it a lot, and aside from that you didn't do anything wrong. I know you were just trying to protect your cousin."

She folded her daughter into a rare hug, making Nicole's further efforts to hold back her tears futile. She cried on her mother's shoulder, wishing Gail could be as understanding.

"When I think about Gail and that man . . ." Her mother's sentence dangled, but the shudder that followed shook both of them.

"Here all this time your father and I thought Gail was the responsible one. We didn't give you enough credit, Nicole. We want you to know how proud we are of you, and how much we admire you for doing the right thing. I know it wasn't easy."

Nicole broke free and took a step backward. Her parents were proud of *her*? Her parents admired *her*? She could barely believe her ears.

"It wasn't easy. Gail hates me now, you know."

"She'll get over it," her mother soothed. "When

this settles down, and she realizes how much you risked to help her, she may even thank you for it."

"I'm not going to hold my breath."

Gail might get over losing her job at Wiener-ageous—who wouldn't?—but what about losing her boyfriend? That had to cut a lot deeper.

Her mother hesitated. "So, did you see all your friends at work when you picked up your check?"

"What friends?" Nicole asked, surprised.

"You must have friends there."

"Mom, we're barely even allowed to *talk* to each other. I don't know what you and Dad think that place is like, but it isn't summer camp."

"Would you like to quit?"

Would she! Nicole opened her mouth to shout her answer to the rooftops, then slammed it shut again. It could be a trick question.

"Because your father and I were thinking it might be better if you did. If you want to," her mother added quickly. "We're not going to force you, of course. But after everything that's happened, it might be better to start fresh somewhere else."

"I *do* want to quit—more than anything. I still have another check coming to pay for that vase, and if I have to I'll get another job. But not there. Not *anywhere* they make you wear a uniform."

Maybe at a clothing store, she thought, her mind

spinning with the thrill of impending freedom from Wienerageous. *Someplace where they appreciate a person's style instead of trying to squash it.* She hadn't been fired, so her employment record was clean. . . .

Her mother held up the paycheck. "I am going to keep this, because the whole point of that job was to teach you a lesson about what things cost. I think you learned more than what we'd intended, though. Some things cost more than money."

Nicole nodded mutely, thinking of Gail.

"As far as I'm concerned, we're even now." Her mother smiled a little. "Keep your next check and buy something nice. It will be the last one—from that place at least."

"Thank you!" Nicole exclaimed, hugging her mother again.

She couldn't believe her luck—not only did she get to keep some of her money, she was leaving Wienerageous. She could have a life again! No more riding buses to Mapleton, reciting stupid slogans, and washing that horrendous uniform. She'd have all the time in the world to win Courtney's friendship back and cut Emily out of the picture.

Or I could try to get along with her, she thought, feeling very virtuous. *I suppose she's not that bad.*

Nothing seemed as bad as working for Mr. Roarke.

Except maybe having Gail so upset with me, Nicole remembered as she climbed up the stairs to her room.

Her mother's letting her off the hook hadn't helped her any there, and it still upset her to think how miserable she'd made her cousin.

All that same stuff probably would have happened to Gail even if I hadn't been there, she rationalized. *She was taking food before I came, and it's not my fault Mr. Roarke finally caught her.* The only thing Nicole had done was tell her parents.

That's all? she thought. *That's plenty.*

As happy as she was about the conversation she'd just had with her mother, Nicole still couldn't help wondering whether it might have been better if she'd never opened her mouth. Maybe Gail really *had* been handling things. Maybe Mr. Roarke wasn't the threat Nicole gave him credit for being. Maybe if she'd looked the other way, the whole thing really *would* have taken care of itself.

Nicole threw herself down on her bed, wishing she knew.

Had she *really* done the right thing?

"Are you sure you don't want me to drive you up to the house?" Aunt Gwen asked, facing Melanie from the driver's seat. "I don't like the idea of dropping you off in the middle of nowhere."

"It's not nowhere." To keep from being spotted by her dad, Melanie had asked her aunt to stop at the intersection between the main road and the

Andrewses' private one. "Besides, I have hardly anything to carry. This is easier."

"It's no trouble at all just to drive to the end of—"

"It's easier for *me*," Melanie interrupted, willing her aunt to take the hint.

"Oh. Well. Will you call me, then? Soon?"

"Sure." Melanie hesitated, not sure if her aunt expected a hug or kiss or something. In the end, she settled for hiking her gym bag high on her shoulder and simply waving good-bye. "Thanks, Aunt Gwen. See you later."

Her aunt still didn't look too happy about not taking her to her door, but she waved back before she drove off, leaving Melanie alone on the silent corner. Overhead, the clouds were closing in, threatening snow. Melanie shivered and began walking toward her house. Everything she had packed was in the gym bag over her shoulder except for a last-minute gift from Kathy Kelly. That she carried in both hands to avoid crushing the bow.

Kathy had run out to press the package on her as Melanie and her aunt were pulling out of the driveway. "Don't open it until you get home," she'd instructed, her cheeks flushed red from the cold. "And whatever you do, don't lose it."

"I'm not going to lose it," Melanie had answered, laughing. And since she could tell it was a book by the feel of it, Kathy's instruction to open it later didn't leave her burning with curiosity, either. Now she turned it over as she walked, examining the brightly colored paper and wondering what kind of books Kathy liked to read.

The concrete house was quiet when Melanie let herself in. Her steps clicked on the cold marble floor, the sound echoing through the deserted two-story entryway.

Way to welcome me home, Dad, she thought, annoyed that he couldn't be bothered to greet her even after a three-day absence. She'd told him she was staying at a friend's house again, but now she almost wished she'd had Gwen pull into the driveway and lean on the horn, just to get a rise out of him.

The gym bag in one hand, the book in the other, Melanie dragged herself up the curving marble staircase. She didn't know if she was more tired from the emotions of the weekend or the long drive home from Iowa, but the last bit of strength seemed to drain from her body as she walked through the doorway into her bedroom. Tossing Kathy's gift onto her bed, she walked into her closet with the gym bag, intending to separate out the dirty laundry and put everything else away. She had barely unzipped the bag, however, when she lost interest in the project.

I'll do it after my shower, she decided, wandering back into her room and gazing around in a trance.

Mrs. Murphy, the housekeeper, had been there, making everything look too perfect to touch. Melanie crossed the freshly vacuumed carpeting to her windows and looked out over the front of the Andrewses' property. The sky was gray and forbidding, but there were hours before darkness.

What should I do? she wondered. It was still early enough to call a friend and suggest a movie or dinner, but Melanie couldn't think of anyone she wanted to call.

Well, there is one person, but the whole world will freeze over before I make that call.

If she were still in Iowa, she and Kathy could walk down to the footbridge, or maybe even venture farther. Aunt Gwen had promised to take her all kinds of places too, the next time she came back. They had done a little more driving around that weekend, but the weather had kept them mostly indoors. Snowbound, Melanie had half expected her aunt to invite her grandparents over or propose a trip to their house, but the subject had never come up. At the time Melanie had just been relieved, but now she wondered about their absence. Were they still out of town? It seemed like Gwen would at least have mentioned them.

Sighing, Melanie left the windows and walked

back toward her bed, where the bright paper of Kathy's present caught her restless eye. She picked it up and plucked a gift card from beneath the bow, popping the seal with her thumb.

Inside was a handwritten message:

Melanie —
Your mother hid this at my house when we were just teenagers. I've kept it all these years, knowing she wouldn't want her parents to read it, unable to throw it away. Maybe it would be better if you didn't read it either, but if anyone should have it, it's you. I hope I've done the right thing.

Lisa Kelly

Melanie was astonished. In a rush, she ripped off the paper. The book was a diary!

"I can't believe it," she whispered.

Bound in red leather, the diary had gold-edged pages, with a leather strap and brass buckle to lock the covers shut. There was no key.

She fumbled with the lock, trying to pull the strap loose, but it didn't budge. Overcome with impatience, she ran to her desk for a pair of scissors, and with shaking hands took them to the strap that held the book closed.

Cutting the leather wasn't easy, but Melanie kept at it, sawing away until at last the strap was severed. She could barely control her trembling as she opened the cover and turned to the first page:

This Book Belongs to Tristyn Allen
Keep Out!

Find out what happens next in Clearwater Crossing #12, *Hope Happens*.

About the Author

Laura Peyton Roberts holds an M.A. in English from San Diego State University. A native Californian, she lives with her husband in San Diego.

Hope Happens

Everyone knows cars and alcohol don't mix, don't they? Sadly, no. Someone in Clearwater Crossing foolishly decides to get behind the wheel after having a few drinks, and the results are tragic. One heart-wrenching accident will change the members of Eight Prime forever as they realize that having faith is one thing . . . but truly believing is another.

Coming in December 1999!